W9-CJC-518

Schaeffer Brown's Detective Fundamentals

A MYSTERY NOVEL

by
Candace Katz

International Standard Book Number: 0-938572-46-6
Library of Congress Control Number: 200592888346

First edition printed 2005
Printed in the U.S.A.

Published by *The Bunny and the Crocodile Press*

Cover photograph by Jonathan Katz
Typography by Barbara Shaw
Printing by Kerry Klear, *Printing Press. Inc.*

Orders: schaefferbrown@monad.org

To Violet and Harold

With love and gratitude to
Wendy, Jonny, Harry, Cindy, and Grace.

Prologue

I WOKE UP in the semi-darkness and groped for the light. It wasn't where it ought to have been on the table beside my bed, and, as my eyes became accustomed to the gloom, I saw a faint glimmer through the window to an unfamiliar courtyard. I roused myself and got out of bed, putting my feet on some cold and sticky linoleum, took two steps, and reached up for the pull cord on the ceiling light.

I knew where I was. A hotel room in Oaxaca, Mexico. The room was papered with limegreen plastic, stamped with the shapes of unconvincing olive-green roses. The floor was darkgreen squares. An unidentified crawling object scuttled past. The room had a bed, a dresser, a closet, and an attached bathroom that I declined to enter. "Hotel Casa Paradiso"—not.

Why was I here, at this unpalatable end of the earth, at this godforsaken hour, alone and claustrophobic and about to be the Mexican equivalent of road kill? How had it come to this?

1

Freefall

LOSING ONE HUSBAND, Oscar Wilde must have said, is understandable; losing two is sheer carelessness. And I was on the verge of losing number two. My first husband was a labor lawyer, who used his not-inconsiderable skills as chief attorney for the Teamsters Union. This position requires a lot of pretty hostile arguing, in court and out. But lawyers like that. To a lawyer, life is adversarial, a fight to the death. Lots of testosterone, which had obvious advantages, of course, but is extremely wearing in the long run. I felt that our life together was a series of gladiatorial combats: he holding a large pointed trident and some spiked knuckle rings; I had the net and the Christian attitude of martyrdom. Our divorce lawyers parted amicably, and I was left with a trove of lawyer jokes of which my favorite is this: What do you have when you have a lawyer buried up to his neck in cement? Answer: Not enough cement.

Now husband number two, Nick, who is the impetus for the first part of my story, was entirely different from my first husband. Nick was English and a banker working at the CitiBank in the main Washington office. At least I could have sworn that Nick was entirely different, but then, when he opened his raincoat, as it were, he turned out to be exactly the same. What was there about me that attracted cold, aggressive, uncaring men? And, more to the point, what was there about me that liked them? I guess I didn't realize that Nick was like that right away. He was actually the most alive man that I had ever met. Childlike, he loved holidays and celebrated all of them—from lavish, twinkling Christmases filled with gifts and fresh fir trees and snow to Midsummer Night, a time for cucumber sandwiches, strawberries, and champagne.

But over time, I saw the darker side of Nick. Brilliant at his work, he had a unique view of things and was usually right. By the same token, he needed, could not psychologically afford, to ever be wrong. How could I know that he would come to scornfully dismiss my opinions? That he would lash out in anger—breaking glasses, hurling chairs against the wall—if his self-esteem were threatened by an off-hand remark or carefully worded criticism? That he would punish me with silences that would last for days? That ultimately I feared that he would hurt me?

And what did I do about it? Nothing. Little by little I became meeker and more fearful of offending and having his wrath, or almost worse, his brooding silence descend on me. Slowly, my sense of self-worth eked away, leaving me fearful, and vulnerable and unlovable.

I would analyze this situation *ad nauseum* with Rachel, my best friend and feminist lawyer. A confirmed non-marrying type herself, she scorned and pitied my sad psychological condition.

"Why am I so pathetic?" I would ask her plaintively over some mild orange chicken at P.F. Chang's. "Beats me," she would answer, savoring her beer-battered pan-fried shrimp. "You used to have guts."

"Right," I would say, brightening a bit. I would reminisce: "Remember the time when you and I hitchhiked across France with a group of French students and played big band music for our supper?" This was in graduate school. Rachel and I went back a long way.

But Rachel was right. I hadn't always been like this. I was plucky, had spunk, was playful, even daring. I acted in plays in college, undertaking Shakespearian pages with wrinkly tights and Noel Coward heroines. I was tear-gassed and arrested in protests and delighted in seeing myself carted away on the evening news. I smoked what was handed to me and had several lovers not—as Chaucer would have said—at chirche door. I was enterprising, too. I got my Ph.D. in English literature and taught at NYU before I moved with Nick to Washington.

I was, in former days, lively and passionate. I loved literature and language and words. I had an insatiable curiosity about people. Everyone was fascinating to me. I watched movies like an addict. I collected Elvis memorabilia (long story) and anything having to do with cows. I skied when I got the chance and played tennis when I didn't. I liked to cook, mostly Julia Child's French recipes, and feed people. I loved to travel and absorb the local food and color—be it Memphis, Tennessee, where I gorged myself on Elvis-approved fried banana and peanut butter sandwiches, or Santa Monica, California, where I went vegan, drank carrot juice, and stopped in an oxygen-inhaling health bar.

But, alas, something unfortunate had happened to me when I married both times: Unaccountably, I grew meek and cautious and dependent. I lost my sense of adventure, my sense of self. I had, in fact, become what the wise courtesan Millamant dreaded in Congreve's *Way of the World*: I had dwindled into a wife.

"It's not only your personal life that's so pathetic," Rachel would add, chewing thoughtfully. I loved the way she piled on. Only old friends were allowed to do that. It was therapeutic. "Instead of choosing a career and sticking with it, you keep trying them on like shoes on sale."

I couldn't deny it. I had showed pretty much the same bad judgment in picking careers as in picking men. They seemed to keep evaporating before my eyes. I had left my job at NYU only to move to Washington as noted above; then I snagged a great job for a liberal Congressman from Rhode Island, but he decided not to run again; and finally I had found a really good position at the National Endowment for the Arts, and I worked there happily, giving away grant money to worthy poets and the like—until the agency was downsized and the last hired (me) were first fired.

So here I was about to be jobless again and at the same time about to be husbandless—I suspected—for the second time. What was I doing wrong? A vast need for security and no sense of commitment, or simply the worst judgment since Richard Nixon? Or was it indeed a carelessness about my life? A feeling that it didn't count for much, which was just more bad judgment. Instead of it feeling like the first day of the rest of my life, I felt as though I were hitting another dead end, and thinking that this time I'd fallen and I couldn't get up. You know, when you ski and do a face plant in the snow in such a way that you're facing down a steep hill, and your skis are pointed in different directions, and your upper body strength isn't quite what it should be, then you might get a sense of how I was feeling then. You think that you just might as well lean back in the snow and wait to die.

(There actually are some dead people in this story, even if you don't count the psychologically dead ones like me. But I am getting ahead of myself.)

As I was saying about my marriage to Nick, over the last few months, our relationship had been wearing pretty thin. We hardly saw each other and had little to say when we did. Gone was the happy sharing of daily anecdotes and conversation. I started moping about the house, looking in a desultory manner at the want ads. Then Nick started coming home really late. I wasn't surprised, therefore, in fact, it almost seemed fitting when I began to suspect that Nick was stepping out on me. Why shouldn't he be? There was hardly even a person to come home to, I was so depressed and despondent. But unbelievably, instead of feeling grateful that the end was in sight, I was filled with rage. I wanted to know for sure what Nick was up to. Like a wife on a television soap, I checked collars for lipstick, I looked at credit cards for unidentifiable purchases, and I called Nick at work at odd hours to see if he were there. But he was either too cagey for me or innocent, and I was weak and paranoid enough to believe the former. Finally, I called Rachel up and enumerated my suspicions.

"Sounds like you need a professional snoop," she concluded. She recommended several and I thanked her. I agreed that she was right but I wanted to find someone that no one knew.

"Just give me a couple of explicit photos," she gloated prematurely, "and I'll drag Nick's sorry bottom up and down the Virginia Commonwealth Circuit Court." Rachel was pretty tough and this was no idle threat. I sometimes wished that her feminism didn't go so far as ignoring the usual female grooming, but it certainly struck terror into her legal adversaries.

And that's how I came to the door of Will Thompson Forensic Associates.

There were only three detective agencies listed in the McLean, Virginia, Yellow Pages. I guess I wanted a suburban detective, where the crime was either white collar or silk sheet. I also chose the Will Thompson Forensic Associates because it was the only detective agency without a boxed ad on the adjacent page listing services such as skip traces and domestic matters, and featuring cartoons of large magnifying glasses. Will Thompson Forensic Associates was just a simple name with a telephone number. I liked that.

I called up quickly before I could change my mind and was greeted by a male receptionist with a reedy voice and a Midwestern-Scandinavian intonation, who identified himself as Michael Carr. I told him that my name was Schaeffer Brown. He delicately asked the nature of my problem, and made me an appointment for the next day, asking me to bring along a photograph of my husband. It seemed very everyday, matter-of-fact, and surprisingly unsleazy, more like making a dentist appointment than anything else.

How could I know that this appointment was to be the turning point of my life?

2

Taking Steps

I TURNED UP the next day at ten o'clock trying not to look like an adulteree. I dressed in a black dress, off-black stockings, low heels, and black jacket, with silver earrings that I never change, and a silver choker. I was glad that I had dressed. The person at the front desk, the one with the Midwestern-Scandinavian voice, was adorable. I remembered that his name was Michael Carr, and he had a remarkably cheerful smile for someone in his line of work. He was tallish, well upholstered but not really plump, about thirty-five, I thought, with blondish-red hair that fell over his forehead. He had green-gray eyes and a slightly upturned nose, and a smile that was, as I looked at it more carefully, at once friendly and slightly satirical.

While I waited, I noted with approval that the reception room was kind of stark, but well lit, painted in shades of yellow, with absolutely no Venetian blinds making sinister stripes of black and white as in a 1940s film noir movie. After a while, a kindly-looking, elderly, white-haired lady appeared and consulted with Michael over what appeared to be two vials of blood. She also had the appearance of someone Midwestern: an ample figure, a twinkly eye, and an apron that should have been stained with cherry pie instead of the gory evidence she held in her hands.

In a few minutes, I was ushered into Will Thompson's office. Upset as I was, I noted automatically that he was a strong, attractive man, with grayish-blond hair and very blue eyes. His office was kind of brown and homey, with one wall covered in books. I'm pretty sure that I would have burst into tears, except for his wide smile and warm handshake. He came from around his desk and sat opposite me in one of two cushioned chairs at angles to each other, our knees nearly touching. It was a relief not to have to shout my private misfortunes across a desk, and I began to blurt out that I suspected my husband was being unfaithful to me and wanted to know for sure.

Mr. Thompson paused a moment. "And why do you want to know for sure?"

This wasn't as stupid a question as it seemed. Reasons went swirling all around me. Curiosity? Masochism? A sure way out of the marriage? A better settlement at divorce? A criminal charge? Adultery was still a criminal matter in Virginia.

"I'm really not sure," I was blurting again. "I guess I want closure, finality."

"Well," said Will Thompson reassuringly, "this is a very simple, routine matter, although always somewhat sad for me. You would think I would get used to betrayals and such. But I don't. I like to keep my eye fixed on the thrill of the chase."

"I'll try to think of it that way," I replied skeptically.

"Now, this will cost you five hundred dollars per day plus expenses, but with your cooperation and the fact that Nick has no reason to believe that you are on to him, and that he is being followed, I would estimate that we could gather some highly incriminating evidence in, say, three days. I will need a retainer of fifteen hundred dollars to begin."

He walked over to his desk and buzzed Michael. "Can you draw up a standard contract for Ms. Brown?" he said. "Ah," he continued, pulling a fresh folder from a drawer in his desk, "I love the feel of a fresh case file. Now let's get down some basic facts."

I wasn't exactly feeling cheerful, but I couldn't help getting caught up in Will's enthusiasm for the hunt. My helplessness began to recede and the let's-nail-this-creep mentality began to set in.

First Will Thompson got all of the basic information about me and Nick. We had the obligatory discussion of the spelling of my first name, Schaeffer. Then he asked for my Social Security number as well as Nick's. He also got the makes and models of our cars (his a black BMW, mine an old black Jeep), places of employment, previous employment, relatives in the area, close friends, hobbies, local hangouts like bars or restaurants (the point being that if Nick stops off for a drink every night, they could start surveillance there rather than at his work). The fact was that I didn't know anything about Nick's after-work habits except that he arrived home late, later, or latest.

Will looked up from his notes. "Now, if Nick were going to stay in a hotel or motel in town, where do you think he'd go?" I appreciated his tact, and tried to think.

"Above all," I said, "Nick hates sleaze and does not go in for tacky. I think he likes the suburbs more than the city, even though he works in the city, and I think he would prefer a hotel to a motel."

"Too bad," said Will. "Harder to get pictures. But let's see, of the big hotels in the suburbs, there's the McLean Hilton and the Reston Marriott, both large, anonymous and not frequented by locals. Now, do you have any idea who Nick might be seeing? Any suspicions? Any clues?"

"No," I said honestly. "There are always dozens of hangers-on in banking eager to get a toe-hold. And there are other bankers. It could be anyone."

"Okay, here's the plan. We're going to need Michael and Marna—you don't mind, do you?" He flicked the buzzer, and they appeared quickly. "Marna, Michael. Have you met Schaeffer Brown? This is Marna Wood and Michael Carr, my associates."

I shook hands with Michael first. He held my hand longer than was strictly necessary and I took the opportunity to look into his green-gray eyes. After a beat, it became awkward. We needed something to say and Michael came through. "Isn't Schaeffer a kind of beer that they don't make anymore?"

"Don't mind him," Will interjected. "He's from North Dakota."

"I once got a Schaeffer fountain pen for high school graduation. I don't think that they sell them anymore either," mused Marna Wood. She shook my hand briskly.

"I don't know what her excuse is," Will laughed. "Marna's from Minnesota. Can we get down to business, guys? We're going to find out what this young lady's husband is up to—if anything." He paused, the introductions over: "Ms. Brown, let's have the picture of Mr. Brown."

I pulled out a snapshot taken by passing Japanese tourists of Nick and me in front of a ruin on the island of Aegina off the coast of Greece. Our arms were around each other and my head was thrown back, laughing. These were happier times. Nick revealed himself in the photo as tall and willowy, a little over six feet tall, with light-brown hair and eyes, a fine aquiline nose, and a fair complexion. He was wearing sandals with socks, which caused a bit of comment from Michael.

"Is Nick American?" he said. "He looks bloody British to me."

"Oops," I said. "I forgot to mention that. He's been here so long. But his English accent has survived intact."

"Cambridge, Oxford, or Red Brick?" continued Michael. "I would guess Oxford, if I had to, though it's an extreme choice."

"Bingo," I answered, impressed by Michael's acuity, though I couldn't see the relevance.

Michael studied the picture carefully and then passed it back to Will and Marna. "Age forty. Drives a black BMW with vanity plates, NUMIS. That stands for?"

"Numismatics. He collects coins," I said.

"He will be leaving the Washington office of CitiBank sometime after seven-thirty tonight," Will continued. "Expected destination, the McLean Hilton or the Reston Marriott. However, we must be on guard for other directions. Mr. Brown has no reason to suspect surveillance, so no need to stay too far behind. Marna, you'll be starting at the Roosevelt Bridge, Virginia side. Wear your hotel maid's garb under your coat, and bring indoor film. Michael, I want you to start at the Dulles access road. I'll start at CitiBank near Fifteenth Street. Of course, we'll be in phone contact throughout. Oh, and Michael, have your Pizza Hut delivery gear just in case."

"Gee," I said on impulse, "This sounds like fun. Can I play too? I can dress like the aggrieved wife."

Will reflected. "Actually, we don't like surprises and almost never take anyone, especially spouses, along unless absolutely necessary."

I looked as sad as I was able. It wasn't sad enough.

"Sorry," Will said. "Television notwithstanding, this is serious business and we can't afford to have an amateur with a grievance helping out."

That stung. I liked these new folks and was starting to feel the old juices flowing again. But I was only a client to them.

Will Thompson assured me that he would call if he had anything to report and in three days' time in any case.

As I shook hands with them and walked out, I had just an inkling that my vital signs were beginning to read slightly higher on the life-force meter.

3

Good News/Bad News

APPREHENSIVE BUT EXHILARATED, I left the Will Thompson offices and headed straight to Bubbles hair salon, in Tyson's Corner. A step like this called for a haircut, and maybe even my first manicure. I decided against the manicure but left with my sandy-blond hair livened up with a few highlights and a shaggier and more devil-may-care cut.

The next thing I did on returning home was to call Rachel. She congratulated me on finally taking charge and told me that the Will Thompson Agency, though small, had a good reputation.

I think that about covers the good news.

At 11:00 a.m. on Friday, the third day out from my first appointment, Michael Carr called me. Sounding businesslike, he asked if I could come in to the office at 4:00 and added that Will had some information for me. I said that I would be there and put down the telephone.

The reality of the situation was beginning to hit me. I hadn't really talked with Nick for about a week, and Will had to have found some evidence of an affair or he wouldn't have to tell me in person. This was getting awfully close to being official.

I dithered around the house dejectedly for a while. I tried to reread *A Girl's Guide to Hunting and Fishing*, which I had liked so much the first time, but I couldn't keep my mind on it. At 1:00, I forced myself to eat my favorite lunch, a toasted cheese sandwich and some Campbell's chicken noodle soup, but it was as dust and ashes in my mouth. Finally, I dressed carefully and drove the fifteen minutes to Will Thompson Forensic Associates, ready to hear some bad news.

Marna Wood was sitting at the front desk this time. Her solicitous expression confirmed the worst. She called into Will to let him know that I was there. Then she called Michael and we all filed into Will's office together.

Will shook my hand and asked me to sit down. The bottom line, he told me, was that he, Michael, and Marna had found evidence of Nick's having an affair, ample enough to hold up in a Virginia court.

"To prove adultery in Virginia, all you have to do is to show time, inclination, and opportunity. What that reduces to is a few suggestive photos and some soiled sheets."

I was stunned by the graphic description and the sordidness of it all.

"But how did you find out so fast?" I gasped, stalling for time, trying to take it in.

"It was almost too easy," Will said. "For three nights I followed Nick and last night Norma picked up his car going on Spring Hill Road towards Route 7. We followed him to the parking lot at the McLean Hilton, and with a telephoto lens I took a few pictures of Nick leaving his car and going into the hotel. Michael watched him check in, noted the room number, and rode up on the elevator with him and several other passengers. It's easy to do when the person doesn't think he's being followed."

I sat staring, tying to make believe that what he was saying had nothing at all to do with my life.

"Then Marna went to the door of Nick's hotel room with her generic housekeeper uniform and some extra towels and snapped a picture when he opened the door. When Nick and company left, Norma took samples of body fluids for DNA testing. But we won't have to go that far. The photos will do. Case closed."

I was really sorry that I had asked for the details.

"There, there," said Marna, patting my knee. "It really is best to know and not just to wonder."

Will went on: "I will mail this material to your lawyer if you like, or you can keep it. I don't really advise you to look at it."

I agreed and gave them Rachel's address. I suddenly realized that I wasn't feeling too good.

"There is one more thing that you ought to know," Will continued. (Wasn't this enough? I thought to myself. Can't I make him stop?) "And I'm afraid that this is going to be a shock to you," he went on relentlessly. "We found Nick with a young man, not with a woman."

I was stunned. This was impossible. How could a person that I had been married to, that I had shared bed and board with for years, seem to be one thing and turn out to be entirely different? How could Nick be a philanderer two ways? I felt humiliated. I felt appalled. And I thought of AIDS.

I must have begun to look very pale.

"I'm sorry for the news," Will said with compassion. "I know that it must be an awful shock. This is truly the worst part of my job."

Marna got me a paper cup of water, which I sipped carefully.

"Let me drive you home, Schaeffer," Michael said. "It's time for me to leave anyhow and you can pick up your car tomorrow."

I managed to thank them all for their good work and shook hands with Marna and Will. Then I put on my coat and let Michael lead me to his car.

"Schaeffer," Michael said, after a long silence as he followed the directions to my house, "are you feeling any better? It will be all right, you know. You're better off without Nick." He trailed off. "I wanted you to know, Schaeffer, that I like you. I'd like to ask to see you again, but I'm in a sort of committed relationship...."

"Thanks, Michael," I said, knowing only that he sensed my gaping vulnerability and wanted to comfort me. Or had Michael felt the spark between us that I had felt?

"I'm glad I told you," he said as we got to my stairs, "because I think you could use a hug, and I don't want to get slapped."

He clasped me hard, and our big coats nestled together. I put my cheek against his for just one moment. It was as soft as mine.

4

Starting Over

◗ WELL, after that fateful night, nature and the laws of Virginia took their course. I had the photos that Marna took—along with the establishing shots that Will got—sent to Rachel, my friend and lawyer. (I couldn't believe that the other man in the photo was Roger from Accounting… but, then, why not? He was cute in a young Leonardo de Caprio sort of way.) Rachel had a quiet talk with Nick's lawyer, who had a quiet talk with Nick, and soon it was all over but the paperwork. Rachel didn't even need to bring in the DNA evidence garnered so carefully by Marna or to brandish her uncared-for legs. This time my settlement was as good as possible, taking into account that our mutual assets were modest.

We sold our house in McLean and I bought a much smaller one in North Arlington, a tiny cottage made of wood painted yellow, all nooks and crannies and very cute. I felt good about having only my things around me. My two most treasured possessions were prominently displayed: a five-foot-high wooden angel of unknown origin that might have come from the prow of a ship, and my beautiful antique wooden hope chest, where I kept my cow collection and other memorabilia.

I didn't see Nick. What did we have to say to each other, after all? I hoped that he was going home to England, but didn't know for sure.

I wasn't actually desperate for a job, but I was going to need one mighty soon, and it behooved me to think carefully about what an unemployed Ph.D. in British literature, recently fired from a government position, could do. I might have gotten a part-time job at Northern Virginia

Community College, but the pay was abysmal and there were no openings anyway.

As the days wore on, I got more and more frightened and began to suffer from a condition I call Loss of Nerve, or L of N, a syndrome perpetually lurking above me and threatening to land. As soon as I woke up in the morning, L of N was with me. You have no husband, no job, no prospects, it said. It was right. I couldn't argue with that.

Rachel called me one night when I was at low ebb to see how I was and why I hadn't called. I tried to explain my state of helplessness, but Rachel would hear none of it.

"This is the best thing that ever happened to you," she said, somewhat exaggerating, I thought. "Nick was a jerk, an upper-class British one at that. You're lucky to be rid of him."

"And my job?" I countered. "Am I lucky to be among the unemployed as well?"

"Well," Rachel said, "at least it gives you a chance to decide what you really like to do. I never saw you as a government bureaucrat anyway."

"Government-bureaucrat bashing is out," I replied. "And what's wrong with a well compensated job with good benefits where you get to help the public?"

"Too dull," Rachel said. "Not you. You like adventure. Crave excitement."

"Are you sure you're counseling the right unemployed person?" I was skeptical.

"Of course. That's why you hook up with all these unsuitable men. You need to feel alive and think that feeling pain is the closest you'll come."

I had to admit that Rachel had a point there. If only I could channel this need for drama in a more positive direction. I invited Rachel to see my new yellow cottage on Saturday brunch and said good-bye. That's when I began thinking about the Will Thompson Forensic Associates.

I called over there the very next day. Michael answered the phone as usual and when I gave my name, he sounded glad to hear from me. He asked me if I needed any more pictures of the scum bucket I called my better half. I laughed and told him that I hoped that Nick was back in Britain looking for some other Colonial to romance with his fancy accent. I told him that I was actually looking for a job and hoping to speak with Will about it. Michael made an appointment for the next day.

I dressed up again in my black skirt, black camisole, and the usual black jacket, black stockings, and clunky black shoes, the Washington uniform for morning, noon, and night engagements. This time Marna was at the front desk doing a Sunday *Times* crossword puzzle. I was disappointed not to see Michael there, but I was glad to see Marna. She gave me a big motherly hug and inquired politely about the whereabouts of my ass of a husband. For a matronly sort, Marna had a decided edge.

I was soon ushered into Will's office. He was winding up a call, and I had a chance to study him more closely. I could see that he was of medium height and strong build with a very tanned complexion that flushed even redder when he became even a little agitated.

His Iowa University degree hung proudly on the deep-brown wall behind him. Next to the diploma was a picture of a small and not very picturesque family farm, with a windmill on one side and a twelve-year-old boy in overalls carrying a heavy pail—perhaps of slop to a pigpen behind him.

Will's hair was shortish, gray, and blond. His eyes were a bright blue, and I thought I could make out the features of the Iowa farm boy in his wind-weathered face.

When Will got off the phone, he turned and grinned at me and his teeth showed nicotine-stained and irregular. But it was a great grin and made me feel flushed. I guess when I saw Will last time I had been too upset to appreciate fully his obvious magnetism.

"So you want to be a detective?" he said slowly and quizzically.

"Well," I said seriously, "I need a job, and I need to learn something new, and I think I would be good at this sort of work."

He looked at me as if sizing up a prize sow.

"Do you mind if I have a cigarette?" he said.

I shook my head, and he lit up a filter-tipped Camel and inhaled with relish. This was clearly an aid to thinking.

"I like you, Schaeffer, I do." He paused again. "I've seen a lot of people in tough spots, and I like the way you handled getting out of yours. But I'd rather have lunch with you than make you my assistant."

"I'll take lunch," I said quickly, not stopping to think. "And then I can talk you into this job thing."

Will gave a skeptical half-snort, half-chuckle, logged off his computer, and motioned me to the door. I gave myself a silent high-five sign. For the first time since losing my job and second husband, I began to feel the glimmerings of a reborn self-confidence. I thought that this was a job that I could do and do well.

Will took me for lunch to J. Gilbert's, a McLean steakhouse on Dolly Madison, pretty near Will's office, which was just off Old Dominion. J. Gilbert's was dark and wood paneled, giving off a masculine feel. You might go there with other businessmen for lunch, or at dinner perhaps for an assignation with someone other than your wife. The most distinctive thing about the place though was the separate menu for martinis, all stirred, not shaken. They were divided into three types—Vodka, Gin, and Dessert—with names like the Dirty Martini, Mandarin Martini, and Madras Martini. Will opted for the classic dry gin martini and I followed suit, seeing as he seemed to be an expert. Then Will ordered a large quantity of red meat, the ten-ounce Black Angus Top Sirloin, and I did the same. I had a principle of eating the specialty of the house, whatever the house.

After a little small talk, I started my sales pitch, and if I do say so myself, really rose to the occasion. Acknowledging the obvious—that I had no training for work in a detective agency or experience—I emphasized what I hoped would be useful skills: I knew my way around the Internet, I was quick to pick things up, and I could use a camera, read road maps, and was fearless (a lie). I was also, I said, fit, but with my small frame, narrow shoulders, wavy sandy hair, and gray-green eyes, I was highly unmemorable and could blend inconspicuously in any crowd. Also, people trusted me and liked to confide their life stories to me on trains and airplanes; they asked directions of me on the street and offered to save my place in line. Also, I liked to see justice done, and this was a good way to do it. Mostly, I concluded, I was eager (read desperate), enthusiastic, and would work dirt-cheap.

Will gave his trademark chuckle in response to this pitch. He asked me some questions about my past and my other jobs; he told me a little about his. Over the drinks, lunch, coffee, and another filtered Camel for Will, we decided that we liked each other.

How two such people, born and bred such different places and ways, could come to share most major values amazed me. I grew up in an academic family in Connecticut and went to college at Columbia University in New York; Will was brought up a Methodist on a farm in Iowa with no near neighbors, and was the first in his family to attend college. Yet we were both liberals, agnostics, and cynics with soft hearts. Somewhat surprisingly to both of us, I think, we were starting to become friends.

"You really want this job," Will asked, I thought a little wistfully, "and not another lunch instead?" He put his hand on my wrist, sort of a cautionary gesture, sort of a tentative caress.

I was torn for a moment. His eyes were very blue. He looked worn, and a little dissipated, but I could see that Iowa farm boy underneath. He must have been a really cute kid, and a super cute college student; he practically still had a cowlick. But there were lots of men, I guessed, to have lunch with. Michael Carr included, I thought to myself. And besides, who needed men? Hadn't I just decided to swear off them for the foreseeable future? My heart was raw. It didn't need further pummeling.

"I want to work with you," I said finally, in as much of a businesslike tone as I could muster.

"All right," Will said slowly. "You start Monday, minimum wage till you can pull your weight. You work with me and fill in as needed. We revisit this arrangement at the end of three months."

I nodded.

"This business is everything to me. I don't have children. I no longer have a wife. My mother and father still live in Ames, Iowa, and they're proud of me, but I'm the son who got away...."

I waited.

"If you work for me, I demand your loyalty and only one other thing."

"Okay," I said cautiously.

"I want you to promise that you will always tell me the truth. I can see that you're the type that would try to spare someone's feelings. But I can take the truth, and I need to know that you'll be honest with me."

"I promise," I said.

And we sealed the deal with a firm handshake.

5

Steep Learning Curve

ON MONDAY, I showed up early, wearing my black suit with white camisole and off-black stockings, and looking serious. Will was sitting at the front desk, drinking coffee, smoking a filtered Camel, and talking on the phone. He motioned me in, all business, and I guess I felt a little twinge of regret about what I had passed up.

Marna and Michael soon followed, wiping the fall rain off their feet and hanging up their coats. They both had been told that I was coming on board and were clearly enthusiastic about getting more help, although both noted that I had precious little experience.

"And," said Marna, who acted as Compliance Officer for the firm, "you need eighty hours of training to register as a private investigator in the Commonwealth of Virginia. Till then, you can only be office gofer." The Compliance Officer makes sure that a detective firm follows all of the rules.

"Fine," I said, happy as a clam. And in truth, I think all three were happy, too.

So that's how I came to be with Will Thompson Forensic Associates. As I got to know the place better, I realized that each of the detectives had his or her specialties. Besides being resident grandma and Compliance Officer, Marna kept the books and was an expert in blood work, fingerprint analysis, and crossword puzzles, about which everyone in the office was very competitive. Michael was the resident computer hacker and encryption specialist. His hobbies were Irish poetry, world beat music, and learning everything about breaking codes. Will simply knew everything.

And while I wasn't yet pulling my weight, I was getting smarter. I enrolled in the Private Investigator course at Northern Virginia Community College for 80 hours of instruction, plus three papers, and a lengthy fill-in-the-blanks exam. Passing this course, along with passing an FBI computer check of my fingerprints for major felonies, plus a $76 check made out to the Department of Criminal Justice Services in Richmond, VA, would get me a Private Investigator's registration, renewable yearly for $35 dollars with eight hours of in-service training every two years.

The 13-week, one night a week class was great. Most of the instructors were retired FBI men (and I do mean men), each specializing in a different aspect of detection-surveillance, camera work, interviewing, collecting evidence, writing reports, criminal law in Virginia. It surprised me that they did not all resemble the deadpan, taciturn FBI men of TV fame—no, they seemed to enjoy the sport of their profession, the dress-up, make-believe, gadgetry, and cops-and-robbers ploys. The students in my class were all recently fired in the government downsizing, retired, or about to be, and looking for second careers like me. Many of them were policemen tired of the force. Everybody knew a lot and was eager to share. Not to make this sound too much like Nancy Drew, however, I should say that the topics we discussed—how to recognize child abuse, how blood stains spattered on a wall, for example—were grisly enough, the crimes real, and the consequences weighty.

Meanwhile, I had been gofer par-excellence at Will Thompson Forensics Associates. I was good at being patient, observant, and losing myself in a crowd. I was really bad at following a car on my own without being stopped by the police (which cost us a lot in one investigation) and sweeping up tiny bits of evidence into plastic bags (no fine-motor skills). I was good at getting people to trust and confide in me, but, too trusting by nature, I needed more experience in knowing when people were lying.

We had our good days, of course, like when the child-abandoner with only a P.O. box in Omaha finally used the "free promotional phone card" that we had sent him, thus revealing his whereabouts. We had our bad days, too, like when the Family Court judge didn't buy our case of child neglect, even when she read the inventory of ninety-nine beer cans laboriously retrieved from the garbage bins of the father in question and meticulously chronicled. Or when the "businessman," to whom Marna and I were delivering a summons, opened fire on us with a B-B gun. But I was gaining experience and learning a lot. With the Will-Marna-Michael team as mentors, I was really coming on.

Hands down, not-even-close for my worst day, was the day the letter bomb arrived.

Michael and I were alone in the office at about 11:00 a.m. Except for Will, we all shared the scutwork of the office. Well, maybe as a newbie, I got a little more than my share. In any case, it was my turn to sit receptionist, answer phone calls, and open, log in, and sort the mail. There was the usual junk mail, of course, plus solicitations, bills, payments, *P.I. Magazine*, the envelopes of which I slit open with a letter opener, and sorted into neat piles for logging in.

And then there was a smallish box just addressed by hand to Will Thomson's Forensic Associates. The return address was smudged and illegible as if the ink had run, but the postmark read Washington, DC. I shook the package in a gingerly manner. It wasn't ticking or anything obvious like leaking white powder, but we really don't get many packages like that. In truth, I was a little suspicious, but since I spent a good deal of my time at the office trying not to look stupid or scared (particularly in front of Michael), I thought that I would just treat the package like regular mail.

I didn't want to come running for help every 15 minutes. What the hang, I told myself, it's probably some Godiva chocolates from a grateful client.

But something told me that the box looked funny, and I held it up to my ear again, thought maybe I had heard something after all. Just then, Michael came up from behind me, and took the situation in with a glance.

"Christ Almighty, Schaeffer," he shouted at me. "What the hell are you doing?" He ran toward me, grabbed the box from my hands and simultaneously hurled it into the farthest corner of the reception room. At the same time, Michael knocked me off my chair and pushed both of us under the desk.

To my horror, the package exploded instantly when it hit the floor with a hideous frightening noise.

"Good God," Michael hissed at me, shaking me by the shoulders. "Don't they teach you anything in that damned detective course of yours?"

Very much shaken and very much ashamed, I started to cry, which made me feel more ashamed. We were still under the desk. Michael softened and put his arms around me, this time rocking me back and forth a few times.

"Hey, never mind," he said. "There's a first time getting a package bomb for everybody."

"Thank you," I said, snuffling a bit, but I'm not sure that the words actually came out.

"It'll be okay," Michael continued to comfort me. "You've just got to be a lot more careful. It's not all just fun and surveillance, you know."

I tried to smile back, but I couldn't. I swear that until that moment the danger of my newly-chosen profession had not sunk in. Had I opened that package, I could have lost my eyes, my face, my hands, my life. In a way, the latter sounded preferable. All the plastic surgeons in McLean, and there are many, wouldn't have been able to put me together again.

We stood up to survey the damage, which was considerable.

"But who would have sent this? Who was it meant for?" I asked in shock.

"Hard to say. Unfortunately, we have lots of enemies. Especially Will, who's been in this business a long time. You know, people he's helped put away. People who've lost their children in custody battles, were prosecuted for insurance fraud. Who knows?"

I stood there, still stunned.

"I'm going to call the police and then the insurance company. We can give them a statement. The police may be looking for a package bomber and we could help them out, or they may be able to tell us someone to watch out for. Anyway, we need the police report for our insurance claim."

By the time a policeman arrived, I was composed enough to describe the package for them, but I couldn't really come up with much. The handwriting, I remembered, was in printed capital letters in blue ink. The return address seemed similar, but was too smudged to make out; the postmark was DC. I felt dumb and dumber as they swept up the debris and said that they would have it analyzed.

Michael decided that we needed a long lunch, so he left a message on the machine, locked up the office, and we headed for J. Gilbert's in his car. I was still too shaken up to drive.

I was finally coming to when we reached the restaurant. "You've saved my life, young man," I said. "Can I buy you lunch and the first martini?"

Michael laughed. Then he turned and kissed me.

6

Personal Matters

THAT KISS really confused me. Well, delighted, and warmed, and confused me. It was something that I wanted, of course. I savored it. I knew that Michael cared about me. But what did it really mean to him? Just that we had been through an awful time together and were still alive, or more?

I found out somewhat sooner than I had expected.

We were seated at a booth near the back of the restaurant. We didn't say much till we had ordered BLT sandwiches for both of us and had taken our first sips of our martinis.

Michael offered a toast. "To life," he said, and we drank again.

"To life sentences," I toasted and was able to smile about it. I was still feeling pretty overwrought, but the martini was just beginning to do its magic work.

"Schaeffer," Michael began with obvious discomfort. "About what I did in the car, kissing you, you know, I'm not sure why I did it. I just... I shouldn't have. I'm living with someone, you know."

"I know," I said. "It's really okay, Michael. It's been a hard morning. It doesn't count."

He smiled at me gratefully.

"So tell me more about this lucky person," I said, hoping, of course, that she was a visiting computer worker from Bulgaria on a six-month visa or someone with a painless but nonetheless terminal disease like in the movies.

"Well, you know that her name is Anna? She's an analyst for the World Bank."

Sounds perfect, I noted glumly to myself. "And how long has this been going on?"

"Oh, ages," he said. "We've lived together for over a year now. It's rock solid, you know. But there's always my job and her job. Every time things seem really smooth, she is assigned a trip somewhere exotic. I don't know."

"Hmm." I said noncommittally, and reinforced my not-caring mood with more olive-flavored vodka. "Why is nothing easy?" I meant me and men, me and Michael, etc., but the comment was open for wide interpretation.

We ate and drank the rest of our lunch quietly; then Michael drove us back to the office.

"Let's shut down for today," Michael said. "I don't have it in me to go back to work."

I took Michael's hand. "I am deeply sorry for putting us both in danger today. I swear that I will be more careful in the future."

That electrical current joined us again until I withdrew my hand. Then I got into my old black Jeep and drove home.

Now, with Michael tantalizingly out of reach, the seal on my personal life officially read "Moribund." I was still feeling emotionally devastated by my breakup with Nick and by the outcome of the infamous night of surveillance. But no more so, it turned out, than Nick himself, who had so readily agreed initially to a divorce settlement. As the story got out about the affair between Nick and young Roger in Accounting at the bank, Nick was deeply humiliated by the revelation, banking being one of the few remaining professions where it doesn't do to be gay. Unfairly, Nick assumed that either I or my lawyer, Rachel, had leaked the information, trying to cause trouble for him. This was in no way true, of course; Rachel and I only wanted my share of the assets and Nick out of our hair. But this obvious truth didn't stop Nick from believing what he wanted to and threatening to sue me for defamation, kill me, or worse. Who knew that he had such a melodramatic streak? Sometimes he would just call me up in the evening and scream at me until I hung up. And many times, I would pick up the telephone only to hear a pause and then a click. Was that Nick, too? The calling and the yelling and the threatening were beginning to unnerve me. As he and I actually communicated only by rumor at this point, as the expression goes, I really didn't know what he was up to, or what his short- and long-range plans were. I fervently hoped that he was finding another continent to frequent where the sun never sets on the British Empire.

Meanwhile, Rachel and I hung out together a lot. Detective hours are hardly nine-to-five. I mean, you're on surveillance or you're not no matter what time it is—but lawyers' hours are like that too. And we liked doing things together. I wasn't ready to date again. Well, unless Michael asked politely. Maybe I would never be. I spent a lot of time puttering around my little yellow house and making it just the way I wanted, primarily with dried flowers and other decorations from Robert Redford's Sundance catalogue. It was wonderful having something of my own.

Mostly, I spent a lot of time on the job and in my night class, finally securing my Private Investigator registration in late fall. I took the paperwork to the Virginia Department of Motor Vehicles the morning I got it back in the mail, in order to have an ID card made up. I was ready for the fact that the ID card would look a lot like a driver's license—but I looked sternly into the camera eye to compensate. I had already purchased myself a flip-open black-leather case to keep the ID in from the police store in Arlington, which I could flash just like in the TV shows. As soon as I got the card back from the Motor Vehicle clerk, I slipped it carefully under the plastic holder and flipped it shut. Gosh, that felt good.

When I got to the office, Marna had organized a little celebration for me. It was just the four of us—Michael, Marna, Will, and me—plus a bottle of whiskey, four glasses and a German chocolate cake from the venerable Heidelberg with a magnifying glass on it. As a graduation gift, Will had also gotten me a key chain, with an eight-inch black wooden cylindrical stick on it. It looked innocuous, but it could deliver a painful blow to the eyes or the company jewels if unexpected. For her gift, Marna had produced a soft case, which she had crocheted herself, to hold a small can of pepper spray or tear gas. I vowed to carry each of these gifts religiously.

Finally, Michael gave me a beautifully wrapped paperback on the history of steganography, which is the art of successfully hiding information in obvious places. The first chapter, for example, told about how the Romans would brand information on the bald heads of messengers and then send them off. By the time they had reached their destination their hair had grown in to hide the message. Only those expecting the information would know to shave the messenger's head. (Crude, but effective, I thought to myself.) Michael's card read, "To a fellow P.I. May all be revealed."

The whole event, the cake, the presents, and especially Michael's card made me feel a bit teary, but, believe me, I didn't let it show. Anyway, I felt well and truly initiated, and very glad to be who and where I was on that late-December day. Lonely? Of course. But private investigators were meant to be lonely. And besides, I was about to help Will on a new and intriguing missing person's case. And I wasn't just a gofer anymore. I had the Private Investigator's ID, in a black leather flip-open case, to prove it.

7

Real Life, Real Guns, Real Bullets

THE NEW CASE involved the disappearance of a teenager from Great Falls, Virginia, one of the toniest of the Washington suburbs, outranking McLean in income, Mercedes, and horses per capita. Will had been called by the missing girl's mother, one Emily Crawford, that morning. At this point, Mrs. Crawford did not want to notify the police.

I had seen the crew handle a few missing teenager cases, and I had studied the procedures in my P.I. class. It was essential to rule out kidnapping or other foul play as soon as humanly possible, and it was expected that P.I.s would work both with the police, who had broad networks, and also Internet groups who helped put out the word on missing children.

But in the end, with foul play ruled out, it turned out that most teenagers disappeared voluntarily, usually running away from what were or at least seemed to them to be intolerable conditions at home. In these cases, a careful and full investigation, usually starting with parents and the teenager's friends, pretty quickly yielded results.

As soon as we had cleaned up the crumbs of the magnifying-glass cake, Will and I were planning to drive out to Great Falls and get the information we needed to start the search. It was a rule of Will's that the owner of the detective agency was always on clean-up crew. This extended not only literally to our frequent parties, but also metaphorically to taking on the hardest and the most dangerous assignments. We all knew that Will would never ask us to do something that he wouldn't do himself, and there was a comfort in that as well as cause for respect in him that we all had. So Will had sent Michael and Marna home early while we cleared up my party and talked about the case.

It was, said Will pensively, a puzzle. Why, for example, didn't Mrs. Crawford come in to see us herself? And where was Mr. Crawford? Didn't he know that his daughter was missing? Or was he missing too? And why didn't they want the police to help even when Will suggested that it should be a joint effort?

We were mulling these questions as we logged off our computers, put on our coats, hats, gloves, and scarves, turned out the lights and locked up. It was a very gray Friday, during that bleak time in late December, after Thanksgiving, that you need to wait out until Christmas. Snow had fallen a few days ago, and was hovering in the air, just threatening to fall again.

Will and I both had our cars parked next to one another beside the office. We decided to take mine because the Jeep, albeit ailing and ancient, had four-wheel drive, good for those icy back roads in Great Falls. It was indeed foggy and icy outside, and a bit of something wet and granular was beginning to fall. I unlocked the driver's side with my key and got in quickly, simultaneously unlocking the passenger side for Will and turning on the defroster in front and back in order to melt a crusty covering that had formed on the windows. The small jets of frigid air plus the windshield wipers were doing little to help the situation. In truth, my beloved Jeep had over 130,000 miles on it, and for the last 20,000 or so had failed to produce much heat on demand. This was why I always traveled with assorted sweaters, blankets, and quilts in the back seat.

After sitting there for some time and listening to Will giving me grief about my car (along the lines of "You probably only need a thirty-dollar repair of the thermostat"), I handed Will my trusty bear-claw glove with attached ice scraper. I also handed him a quilt from the back seat to throw over himself and invited him to work on the accumulated ice from the outside.

As Will got out, chivalrous always, I put on my Paul Simon *Rhythm of the Saints* tape for a little sub-equatorial musical encouragement and reached for a few more of the throw quilts in the back seat for me and Will to wrap ourselves in when he came back. I was just beginning to feel a little more snug when I heard, above the sounds of drum and guitar, the bark of what sounded to me like a gunshot.

Terrified and unthinking, I jumped out of the car and screamed Will's name. Will was slumped over the side of the car near my door and was slipping to the ground. I took the two steps towards him and saw that there was blood on his hair and his coat.

"Will," I said again.

He looked at me what seemed like an age and then slipped to the ground, apparently unconscious.

I hesitated only for a second. Blankets or 911? I decided to take more blankets out of the car, covering him up against the cold and shock. I took the cleanest-looking quilt I could find, a baby's pink one with green kangaroos, and held it tightly to the side of Will's head where the bleeding seemed to be worst. I couldn't believe how much blood there was.

Then I maneuvered my cell phone out of my pocketbook and called 911. I gave the location and the need for emergency help. I held on to Will and to the phone until the McLean Fire and Rescue Squad arrived only a few minutes later.

Two men jumped out of the van and started working on Will with scary but efficient speed; putting on an oxygen mask, sticking him with a needle in his forearm, starting an IV. As I watched the two slip a board under him to lift him onto the stretcher, I had a fleeting thought that if Will were going to die maybe I didn't want to live either. I pushed that thought away and climbed into the back of the ambulance for the ride to the hospital.

We were clearly going to Sibley Hospital in Washington. I found that although it's in Washington, we could get there the quickest from where we were in McLean. It's more of a country-club hospital than a big-city one, though, and I had to wonder what the ER staff would make of Will's injuries.

The ride to the hospital gave me a minute to reflect. I put my hand on Will's and said to him, in case he could hear, "Will, I won't lie to you. I know that you've been badly hurt, but I'll do everything I can to help you get better. And to find whoever did this. And most important, I vow to work as hard as I can to keep your agency going well till you're back in charge." I think I said this out loud. Maybe I only mumbled it to myself. I really couldn't tell. I wasn't thinking too clearly anymore.

As soon as we arrived at the emergency room, nurses took Will away on a gurney and I assume that the doctors got to work on him right away. The ambulance guys had called ahead. I waited in the brightly lit emergency waiting room in the quiet hospital. Few people came in or out. Three young women, probably roommates from American University, arrived, one doubled over, maybe with appendicitis. An older woman was wheeled in by a very old man. She was having trouble breathing, thought it was the medication. It was quiet. I read all of the magazines. At one point, I used my cell phone and left messages for Marna and for Michael to call me, but I knew that I wouldn't hear from them for a while. Marna was on a bus (she never flew) to Dayton, Ohio, where one of her sons lived. Michael was en route to spending the weekend with his parents in a retirement community in Arizona. Why was I so alone?

But not for long. Two detectives from the Fairfax County police were soon at my side, notebooks open, asking me questions that I couldn't answer. Detective Tarentino was broad, dark, large, and cute. He was sympathetic and seemed concerned. Detective Cole was also strapping, about my age, with short dark hair and the appealing manner of a concentration camp matron. As if to challenge my first impression, Detective Cole kindly offered to get me a cup of coffee.

I was expecting their questions, of course, and was ruminating about possible answers continually in the back of my head. Did I see or hear anything unusual before hearing the gun shot? Did I see or hear anything after I got out of the car? Did I see someone leaving the scene of the crime? On foot or in a car? All no.

I kicked myself internally. How could I have been so stupid, so unprofessional? How had I managed to have absolutely no leads, no evidence, no clues? Stupid badge in my pocket. Worthless.

The detectives tried not to make me feel bad about my inability to help them. They assured me that they had interviewed any possible witnesses and had come up completely short. Snow falling, poor visibility, no one out walking. They hoped that forensics would be able to help once a bullet had been extracted. They had not yet located a shell.

Also, they told me that they had conducted their search of my car and the premises, and that I was free to drive it away. And they complimented me on getting help so fast. (Well, duh.)

They asked me, of course, whether Will had any enemies that I knew of, anyone who would want to see him dead. The answer was something that I had also thought about. It's something that detectives and, maybe even more so, ex-FBI men sometimes talk about. Their worlds are, in fact, filled with enemies: people who did time on account of their evidence, or lost wives in divorce cases, or children in custody battles. The detectives that I had met simply had too many potential enemies to give it much thought. They were generally wary, kept their guard up and let it go at that.

Detective Tarentino then asked about current cases, which I declined to answer, and where Will and I were headed when he got shot. I told them that we were going to see a new client in Great Falls, but that I thought that the client's identity was privileged since we were technically on retainer by credit card. Where was Marna the Compliance Officer when I needed her?

Both detectives all but spit at that one, but let it go for the time being. They gave me a number where I could call them and said that they'd be in touch.

While being interviewed by Detectives T & C, I had kept my eye on the admitting nurse's station. I walked quickly back there now and asked if there were any news. "Still in surgery," came the reply.

I sat again. This time I got out my cell phone and called the client, Emily Crawford. A very agitated voice answered the phone, and I explained to Mrs. Crawford that we had had an accident, but would be out in the morning. Would 8:00 be too early?

"For Christ's sake," she said. "My daughter is missing."

"I'll be there at seven-thirty," I said hurriedly and hung up the phone.

About two hours later a surgeon came out, blood-spattered and worn-looking. "Your friend is alive," he said. He told me that Will had been badly hurt, and that a bullet had caused a concussion. Will had not regained consciousness yet. The surgeon didn't know if he would. Like they do in the movies, he told me to go home and come back tomorrow.

I couldn't find any words. I couldn't even face my thoughts. I didn't want to think about how badly this hurt me, how vulnerable I had already become, how much I had to lose. While I had been sitting there for the two hours, I had had time to think about how I was feeling and how I felt about Will. I kept coming back to that fleeting thought when I first understood that Will might die, and I had felt with a rush of feeling, 'that's not good, because I do want to live, but if Will dies, I won't want to live anymore.' The feeling was a little like anger at the unfairness of things. The feeling had slipped away as quickly as it had come.

But how did I feel about Will? Was it gratitude, friendship, loyalty, or love? And if love, was it the romantic variety or the sort of love you have for a father? My own dear father had died many years before. Was I needing someone to fill that place in my life? But then I remembered my strong attraction to Will when I first met him and how I had almost traded in a chance at the job for a chance with him. And then there were my hopeless feelings for Michael. It was all too confusing and painful. I needed sleep and 20 years of therapy.

I called a cab, and numbly went home.

8

The Mother

IT WAS ANOTHER cold day in December, this time a clear one, as I drove out Route 7 West a goodly ways to Great Falls, Virginia, to meet Mrs. Emily Crawford, our client with the missing teenaged daughter. Finally taking a right turn at Towson Road, I headed abruptly into horse country, with winding narrow lanes roofed with trees. I saw vast acreages of grazing land and an occasional well-bred looking animal, swishing his black and wavy tail. It wasn't my country, and I felt a twinge of envy for the horsey set who dwelled in such peaceful and leisured haunts.

It was a pretty long drive through the country and it gave me a chance to sort through my thoughts. I was mostly still numb from the events of yesterday. I had called the hospital early in the morning, but there had been no change in Will's condition. I had spoken with Marna and Michael as well, and had broken the news to them. They had both decided to come home right away. Meanwhile we decided that I would keep Will's and my appointment with Mrs. Crawford, and that they would back me up as necessary when they got back. I had also called the Fairfax Police, but they had nothing to tell me.

It was hard getting up that morning. I felt as heavy and old as I had ever felt. I muttered to myself some half-remembered lines from the poet May Sarton about how she felt like an old camel getting to its knees. But I did get up. I had promised Will.

I finally reached a private road, marked with a mailbox, "Crawfords," and turned onto it. It was narrower, and more winding, and unbelievably long. I passed barns and outbuildings, drove through copses and small woods for about ten minutes until I arrived at a circular driveway in front of a house that looked like a backdrop for a Mercedes ad. Actually, there were several cars and trucks in front of the house; they all looked sleek and chic, but identifying luxury vehicles is not my stock in trade. I parked my mud-spattered black Jeep on the end of the road.

I found the brass knocker on the front door underneath a lavish pine-smelling Christmas wreath and knocked tentatively—it was so very quiet. When no one came, I banged more loudly till someone, who had to be Mrs. Crawford, came to the door. She was about 40, with swingy dark hair cut to chin level, and a kind of darting rodent-like face, her eyes set at a slant, and her chin very small. She was wearing an elaborate, multi-layered workout outfit in blue and white and had a Diet Coke in her hand. At one glance, I knew her to be the kind of rich woman who spent most days spa-ing out with her women friends when she was not riding or undergoing liposuction.

Mrs. Crawford beckoned me in with a hurried gesture. I felt for her. She looked tired and scared. Alone in the big house, she looked as lonely as I felt.

"You're here alone?" she asked somewhat abruptly. It could be construed as rude, but I frankly didn't blame her. She wanted her money's worth, and neither of us seemed to have that much faith that I, on my own, could deliver.

"There's been an accident," I began. "Mr. Thompson is in the hospital, and I am handling his case load for a few weeks."

She stared at me. We were still both standing in the front hall. I could see many gleaming surfaces inside, some warm, but mostly cold: shiny wood floors in the living room bestrewn with tasteful quilted rugs, terra cotta tiles on the floor of the kitchen open to the larger room, with polished granite counters and brass pots hanging from rafters. It was a high-tech country look.

"What happened?" she said finally.

"It was kind of a drive-by shooting. The police have no suspects yet. It happened yesterday. Just before I called you."

She frowned at me and took a sip of Diet Coke. "Okay," she said finally. "But I need to find Courtney NOW." Her concern for Will was less than touching.

"I'll do everything in my power to find her," I said. "And I'll be consulting with Mr. Thompson regularly," I added, in an unnecessary lie.

She led me into the living room, and we sat on one of the most enormous sofas I have ever seen. She kind of collapsed back against one of the arms of the sofa and sobbed quietly. "I haven't heard anything at all. Nothing. Nothing. Nothing."

She sounded like a soggy King Lear, and my heart went out to her.

"Okay," I said gently, pulling out my reporter's pad with my notes based on Will's phone conversation with Mrs. Crawford. "Let's go over what we do know: Your daughter, Courtney Smith, is eighteen, and beginning her senior year at the Madeira School. She's a boarder, and you saw her last at Thanksgiving here, right?"

"Well, we spent Thanksgiving at Vail, Colorado, actually. Courtney, Montgomery, my husband, and I went for some early skiing. Actually, Montgomery and Courtney skied. I went to their wonderful spa...." She trailed off.

"And then Courtney went back to school, presumably until Christmas vacation?"

"Yes, we dropped her off at school that Sunday night. Everything was fine." She paused. "I haven't heard from her since."

"Has her father? Or anyone else?"

"You mean Montgomery, her stepfather? Her real father, Curtis Smith, lives nearby in McLean. But we don't see him much."

"Has either of them heard from her?"

She fiddled with the tassel of the velvet throw pillow. "No. Not that I know of."

I thought that was a puzzling reply, but I pressed on, consulting my notes in what I hoped was a professional-looking way. "I know that you first heard about Courtney's disappearance from Ms. Ashton, the Headmistress, two days ago, when your daughter failed to show up for her weekly weigh-in. Did Ms. Ashton have any idea where Courtney might be?"

"No." Mrs. Crawford was becoming morose and uncommunicative.

"Mrs. Crawford," I continued, "do you know of any reason that Courtney would run away from school? Did she like Madeira? Has she ever run away before? Was there a lot of pressure on her?"

"Courtney is not—how can I say this?—a very serious student. She likes riding and skiing. She's never stuck with anything much, though. She isn't much of a student. She's applied to several two-year colleges for next year." She paused. "She likes, as she says, to party, to have fun. She likes to buy clothes and to spend money. Madeira is not a place of great academic pressure, but even so, she might have found it too much."

"What about boys? Does she have a boyfriend? Someone she could run to or run away with?"

Mrs. Crawford stiffened. "She really doesn't confide in me. She hasn't for a long time. You should ask her school friends. They're all called Jessica, I think."

"Is there anything that you can tell me that might help me find Courtney?" I had observed Will asking an open-ended question after a series of specific ones. Sometimes it got a response if you waited long enough.

After what looked like an inner struggle, Mrs. Crawford just shrugged. I guess I hadn't asked the question right.

"No. Nothing," she said. There was something about her that was subdued, dying, or dead. But how would I feel if my only daughter were missing?

"Will Mr. Crawford be home soon?" I asked.

This remark was greeted with a snort.

"I did tell you that he works at the White House, didn't I? Financial adviser on international trade? He barely comes home at all. Keeping up with all those twenty-somethings."

"Well, do you think I can make an appointment to see him?"

"You can try." She gave me Montgomery Crawford's office number. I also got the numbers for Courtney's father, Curtis Smith, in McLean, and for the headmistress at Madeira. I would have to find the Jessicas on my own.

Before I left, I went to look through Courtney's room. It was a girl's dream, complete with canopy bed with white eyelet canopies, Laura Ashley flowered wallpaper, and creamy matching bureaus and vanity table with a large mirror.

It had been professionally cleaned—I could see the neat-looking vacuum-cleaning marks on the lavender carpeting—but it was kind of a mess. A small suitcase was open with some clothes in it, stacks of sweaters were on a chair. Ski gloves, long silk underwear, and fancy dappled cowhide apres-ski boots were thrown in a corner. Make-up, shampoo, conditioner, gels, mousses, and creams of every variety crowded onto the vanity table. What must have been nearly 50 assorted stuffed animals lay about, on shelves, tables, the floor, and the bed.

There were no books. There was no desk. But there were piles of magazines, *Jane, Glamour, YM, Sassy*, and the like strewn about. A fancy boom box and many CD's sat on a table. I searched through the drawers for diaries (none) or letters (also none). There was nothing really too distinctive about the room, nothing that differentiated Courtney's room from the generic teen's hideaway, except, maybe, a pretty extensive collection of matchbooks from all over the world. Someone had been collecting for her for many years. They came from as far away as Singapore and as nearby as J. Gilbert's, where Will and I had had our first lunch.

I suddenly felt really sad. J. Gilbert's reminded me of Will and how badly he was hurt. Would he be okay? Would he talk again? Walk again? I couldn't bear to think about it. Maybe I did have plans for him beyond work. It was just possible.

I got my mind back to Courtney. The most I could do for Will was to help keep his agency going till he could work again. I had to believe that he would.

As I was leaving, I asked Mrs. Crawford about the matchbooks.

"Oh, Curtis collected them, Courtney's real father. From all over the world. He was CIA, you know. Courtney didn't really care about them, I think. I think she just took one when she wanted to sneak a cigarette."

As I let myself out, I told Mrs. Crawford that I would be back in touch within the next 24 hours and hoped to have some leads. I left her my card with my home number and cell phone on it and asked her to call me immediately if she thought of something or if Courtney called.

The temperature had dropped about 20 degrees in the last hour and the sky had darkened again. The door handle on the Jeep was stiff when I opened it, but thank God, the car always starts. I wrapped myself up with the remaining quilts and started to drive away. I looked back at the house before I drove back down the windy private drive. There was one lone light in the living room. No lights at all by the door.

9

The Headmistress

IT WAS about 8:30 a.m. when I left Emily Crawford's house. I drove quickly to the office, stopping on the way at Starbucks for a large cafe latte and a chocolate chip scone. What a weird fusion of cultures (Italian, Scottish, Tollhouse?) and a darn good breakfast. It helped me to fight against my impulse to just get into bed, pull the covers over my head, and sleep for a week, hoping that all would be well when I got up.

Instead, I started making phone calls. First, I called the headmistress of Madeira School, Ellie Ashton. She agreed to meet me at 10:00 that morning. Next, I reached Montgomery Crawford, Courtney's stepfather, at his office in the Old Executive Office Building. He had not heard from Courtney, was very much concerned, and would meet me at his office at 1:00 today. We could then go down and eat at the White House "mess" (reverse snobbery for "dining room") while we talked. He then asked for my date of birth and social security number. That's the worst thing about going to the White House. You really can't lie about your age if you expect to get in at all. Finally, I made a date for 3:00 with Curtis Smith, Courtney's birth father. He lived in McLean, a stone's throw from the CIA, his old haunt. He hadn't heard from Courtney either and was really worried when I told him what was going on. He expected an international conspiracy at the least.

I hardly had a chance to congratulate myself on my efficiency when it was time to head out to Madeira School and face the always terrible headmistress or principal ("Pal?" Hah!), a figure that haunts the imagination like the wicked stepmother of fairy tales. Cool, serene, repressive, the school headmistress or principal lives in all of our hearts.

As I drove back to the edge of horse country, on Georgetown Pike and through the white wood fences that surrounded the school, I experienced Madeira as a pretty impressive place. Once a finishing school for rich young ladies, it was then wracked by the scandal of a drug-imbibing headmistress who shot her diet-doctor lover (and who could blame her since he had taken up with his nurse?). It had now once again returned to its finishing school reputation—but what did it take to be finished these days? On Wednesdays, the girls had rock climbing and auto mechanics. On Thursdays, they volunteered at day care centers and AIDS hospices. But they still boarded their horses at the school, and rode, English saddle, every day.

The Madeira grounds in McLean are extensive; the buildings, brick and classical. I found Ms. Ashton in a small office of pleasing proportions and very nice light coming in from French windows and overlooking a tamed English garden and countryside views of gentle hills framed by graceful trees. Ms. Ashton was wearing a gray suit with pearls. (Some things never change.) She shook my hand forthrightly and told me how distressed she was by Courtney's disappearance, offering her help and that of the staff.

Ms. Ashton, who was perfect, apparently disliked imperfection in others or any awkward or messy matters that disturbed the harmonious serenity of herself, her room, her school, or her morning in any way. Nevertheless, she was making an effort to be helpful.

According to Ms. Ashton, Courtney was a somewhat immature student, who had suffered greatly by the break-up of her parents' marriage and the remarriage of her mother to Mr. Montgomery Crawford about three years earlier. (Ms. Ashton re-crossed her perfect legs in graytoned stockings and gray low-heeled shoes and reached up to push back a wisp of her elegantly coifed gray hair.) There was something of an instability in the family situation, which, she thought the school environment and friendships there were helping to correct. (Ms. Ashton stared at the soothing country scene out the window.)

When I pressed her, she told me that she knew of no particular problems that Courtney had at school. But she did give me leave to talk to Courtney's teachers, to examine Courtney's room, and to discuss Courtney's disappearance with her two closest friends, Jessica Carter and Jessica Kim. (Ms. Ashton looked up, hopeful that her ordeal was over.)

I thanked her for her help and was getting up to leave when she began reluctantly to bring up a subject that was clearly on her mind.

"You know, Ms. Brown," she said slowly, "Madeira has recently fought its way back from scandal to become an even finer institution for young women than it has ever been."

I murmured my assent.

"It would be sad indeed if this probably innocent disappearance were to find its way to the press. I rely on you, of course, for your absolute discretion."

"I assure you, Ms. Ashton, that my investigation will be carried out with the greatest care and concern for all involved. But finding Courtney is my first and only priority."

"Of course, of course," she answered. "It is the only thing that matters."

10

The Friends

I FOUND the two Jessicas at the late-morning brunch featured at boarding schools on weekends. They were eating at a long table. Jessica C. (as Jessica Carter was known) had straight blond hair and was preternaturally thin. Jessica K. (as Jessica Kim was known) was Korean American, with straight black hair. She was preternaturally thin as well. Both wore incredibly grungy uniforms of baggy jeans and oversized baggy gray sweatshirts over black turtlenecks with distended necklines. Holey sneakers rounded out their ensembles. Here were, probably, two of the richest girls in America. Go figure.

When I came up, they were picking at half-filled bowls of cornflakes and skim milk in a desultory manner. I explained who I was, and the prospect of hearing news of Courtney seemed to perk them up a bit.

"Sorry, girls," I said slowly, "I haven't heard anything from Courtney. I was hoping that you could help me."

Jessica C. and Jessica K. exchanged looks. Then silence.

"This is serious," I said. "Courtney may be in trouble. Her parents are crazy with anxiety. If you know anything about where she is, I'd advise you to spill." (God, it was easy sounding hard-boiled with two adolescent anorexics.)

Again an exchange of glances. Finally, the dark-haired Jessica offered, "I know that Courtney took a taxi to Dulles airport on Sunday morning. We covered for her so no one missed her for a while."

"Did she say where she was going?" I tried not to sound too eager.

The blond Jessica, who had perfected the vacant look, seemed as though she were trying to make up her mind. "Mexico," she said finally.

"Mexico?" I echoed stupidly. "Did she say why? Or where in Mexico? It's a big country, you know."

The dark-haired Jessica had on a highly-honed "well, duh" expression. "She did go to meet someone, but she didn't say who. And she didn't say why. If I had to guess, I would guess a certain Timothy Parker, a senior from St. Alban's, but I couldn't say for sure."

"Motive: sunshine, seduction, and margaritas," added blonde Jessica and giggled.

I felt somewhat relieved. This might not be sinister but only incredibly stupid and irresponsible.

"Okay," I said. "This is really helpful. Now do you have any idea where in Mexico they went?"

"God," said blond Jessica. "I'm not sure I remember. Do you, Jessie?"

Dark-haired Jessica looked vacant. Then a light dawned. "What's the name of the little dog that yaps at your heels a lot?"

"Chihuahua?" I said.

"Yes. That's it!" Pause. "At least I think so," she added. "Is that right, Jess?"

Blonde Jessica thought so too but couldn't be sure.

"When is she coming back?" I asked. "Can I get in touch with her?" But the Jessicas had run out of ideas and information.

"Well, thanks, guys," I said seriously, giving them each the business card I was so proud of. "Call or send me an e-mail if you can remember anything else—or if you hear from Courtney. She still could be in trouble, you know."

From the dining hall, I got directions to Courtney's dorm room. It was in a handsome red brick colonial building, with white door and shutters. I passed a lounge area where young women in clothes similar to the Jessicas' were arrayed in uncomfortable-looking positions on the floor and across chairs and sofas reading large textbooks or watching TV. I vaguely wondered why people weren't sitting at desks and whether their parents were getting their $30,000 per year's worth of education.

I asked my way to Courtney's room and was given directions. Courtney was a senior, so she was allowed a single room, No. 26, which I found up one flight of stairs and along a corridor that was pretty badly lit, to save electricity I guess. I knocked and then opened the door and turned on the light.

The room was spartan: a single bed with a blue plaid comforter, matching sheets and pillow slip, a window, a bureau, a desk, and a closet. An obscenely large Tweetie Bird stuffed animal graced the bed.

Using the technique I had learned from Will, so as not to miss anything, I divided the room into quadrants and began at the left. I checked in and under the bed first. Nothing on the bed but a few more stuffed animals, and that kind of small egg-shaped cyberpet that had clearly been left to die. I looked under the bed and found a pattern of dust bunnies that suggested the recent extraction of a small suitcase. The bureau in quadrant two held nothing of interest. The underwear drawer seemed to have been depleted, but sweaters and turtlenecks were still there, perhaps confirming the destination of a warm climate. The desk, in quadrant three, had a number of textbooks with papers stuffed in haphazardly. I guessed that this wasn't a study vacation.

Finally a payoff: I found a college-ruled yellow pad with nothing on it. I rubbed my hand lightly over the surface for indentations from writing on a previous page as I had seen Will do. Eureka! There were some. I grabbed a number two pencil from the desk and lightly colored in over the indentations. Unbelievably a few letters and numbers appeared. It looked like a "U" and an "S" and then a "342" or "347." Could this be a flight number? U.S. Air? Ignoring the fourth quadrant of the room (would I regret this later?), I walked down the hall to a pay phone, called information, and then US Airlines.

"Can you tell me, please, where U.S. Air flight 342 from Dulles goes?"

The answer, after a requisite amount of computer clicking, came back "Budapest." Somewhat taken aback, I inquired after the other flight, U.S. Air flight 347. Requisite clicking. "That would be Oaxaca, Mexico," the airline clerk replied uncertainly.

"Can you spell that, please?" I demanded. After a little backing and forthing, we mutually agreed the destination was Oaxaca, Mexico, pronounced "Wa-ha-ca."

Did this make sense? The Jessicas had told me "Chihuahua." But between Oaxaca and Budapest...Oaxaca had to be it.

I made a reservation on the next plane from Dulles International Airport, which left the next morning at 7:30 a.m.

11

The Stepfather

FEELING ACCOMPLISHED, nay distinguished, by my morning's work, I drove into the District to make my lunch date at the White House with Courtney's stepfather. I put in my Linda Ronstadt tape and listened to one of the most dismal of country ballads, "Love has no pride, when you call out my name... I'd go down on my knees." I can always gauge my mood by how loudly I sing along. If I can't sing at all, it's rock bottom. This morning I could hum softly.

I parked in a garage on 18th Street and walked along the pedestrian walkway, unattractively set in concrete to the Pennsylvania Avenue entrance of the White House. After much security, picture ID, and bag check, I was checked off on a list and was rewarded with a visitor's pass.

Many scurrying aides, looking roughly age 15, walked briskly hither and thither. These were the people running the country—a comforting thought. I asked the guard to call up to Montgomery Crawford's office, and in about ten minutes Courtney's stepfather came down and introduced himself.

Montgomery was gorgeous. He was large and good-humored-looking with fine features and floppy light-brown hair that fell over his forehead. He, like his wife, looked to be in his forties, but as much as she was pinched and thin, he was portly and expansive. As much as she was silent and forlorn, he was hale-fellow-well-met. Was this her fault or his? They used to say that women don't have accidents, they cause them. In my view, behind every pinched and miserably unsure woman is a carefree and careless man.

Montgomery gently touched my arm in a practiced sort of way and led me to the mess or dining room, pointing out meeting rooms and the corridor to the Oval Office along the way. When we reached the dining room, uniformed, black waiters led us to a good table near a wall. Montgomery recommended the special black bean soup and did a short riff on why the dining room was called the mess (a nautical term) and the diners served exclusively by Filipino waiters. Unfortunately, I couldn't keep my mind on the explanation and it didn't seem to make much sense.

When the black bean soup arrived, I got down to business. I confirmed that Montgomery had found out about Courtney's turning up missing from his wife. Oddly, although Montgomery claimed not to know of Courtney's whereabouts, he did not seem quite so worried as his wife, Emily, who was desperate. Was this just his temperament, or did he lack concern for a recently adopted daughter?

"Courtney's a pretty wild and headstrong young lady," he mused. "She's also boy crazy and hates school. It's more than likely that she's gone off on an early spring break." He paused. "We'll hear from her when her money runs out."

Slightly appalled at his callousness, I seriously wondered whether to trust him with the information that I thought I had. Just generally I didn't trust him either. And Will had trained me not to give information to anyone unless I was very likely to get something in return.

I ate some more black bean soup. It was good, rich, and filling with little ham chunks. I made a snap decision.

"I have reason to think that Courtney went to Oaxaca, Mexico—along with a boy from St. Alban's."

"Really?" said Montgomery noncommittally. "Well, that fits in with my theory. How did you find that out?"

"Oh, the usual way," I said. "You know. Asking around."

He looked thoughtful. "What are you planning to do?" he said finally.

"I'm planning to take the next flight there myself and look for her. Her mother is frantic. Don't you two communicate at all?" I asked meanly.

"Of course we do," Montgomery snapped back, the dig not lost on him. "I've just been extremely busy the last fiew days. You see this place." He nodded his head at the buzzing room around us. "Everything is a crisis."

I nodded. At that moment, a man walked up to our table briskly, and, without introducing himself, spoke softly into Montgomery's ear. I couldn't make out the words, but Montgomery looked really worried. He excused himself and followed the man out of the mess, pulling his cell phone from his jacket pocket at the same time. The man looked like any other white Anglo Saxon Protestant you might see, but he was a lot older than your typical aide and his skin looked toughened by lots of outdoor exposure.

In a few minutes, Montgomery came back and apologized for the interruption without offering to explain it. In any case, he used the interruption to change the subject from our last one on the lack of basic communication between him and his wife. "Who is this boy from St. Alban's Courtney's supposed to be with?" he asked.

I consulted my notebook and came up with the name Timothy Porter.

"Don't know him," said Montgomery. He looked serious then.

"Look, I don't want to seem insensitive, but I don't think that blindly following Courtney to Oaxaca, or wherever she's supposed to have gone, is such a great idea. I would check out the St. Albans boy, give it a few days. Courtney acts out a lot. Likes to drive her mother crazy. I honestly believe that she'll turn up sooner than you think."

He gave me his card, "Montgomery Crawford, Special Adviser to the President for Foreign Trade," and added a number for his cell phone so that I could reach him at any time if I needed to. I thanked him for his card, his information, and for lunch, and we got up to go. Montgomery steered me out the door and to the security checkpoint. As I turned to leave, I handed him my card and asked if he would call me immediately if he got any word of Courtney. He assured me that he would.

"And you'll let me know immediately if you hear anything?" he asked.

"Of course," I said and turned to leave.

I had a few calls to make and one more appointment before I could head back to the hospital to see if there was any change in Will's condition, and I had to struggle to maintain my focus. First, I called the answering service at the Will Thompson agency and asked for messages, of which there were none. Then, I called the McLean police and asked the Inspector on duty for any leads in Will's shooting. Again nothing.

Finally, I called St. Alban's School, a fancy boys' counterpart to Madeira. I think that Al Gore went there. Putting on what I hoped was a 'maiden aunt from Massachusetts' voice, and giving my name as Clarice Porter, I asked if I could speak with Timothy Porter on an urgent matter of family illness. (I figured that he was bound to have some Massachusetts relatives.) The receptionist, gullible as she was, quickly found that he should be in his AP English class, and offered get him and to bring him to the office. It certainly sounded as though Timothy Porter were not in Mexico, but I wanted to hear his voice with my own ears. After about ten minutes of holding and feeding nickels into the pay phone, a young man's voice came on the line.

"This is Timothy Porter. Is everything all right? Who is this?"

I was ready for him. "I'm sorry, very sorry," I replied, still Massachusetts maiden aunt and very flustered. "I was looking for a Thomas Packer. I must have the wrong party. Very sorry indeed."

"No problem," he said, sounding relieved. "I'll give you back to the receptionist."

"Thank you," I said, and promptly hung up the phone. I was out of nickels anyway.

So this was not apparently a romantic escapade as the Jessicas were led to believe.

Curiouser and curiouser.

12

The Birth Father

MY LAST APPOINTMENT of the day was with Courtney's real father, Curtis Smith. He lived in McLean, off Route 123 and close to the CIA, from where he was retired and must have missed badly. I gathered that Curtis was a detail person by the meticulous way he gave directions to his house, using route numbers, street names, landmarks, and compass points.

But when I showed up at 3:00 sharp, I was not prepared for the super-crazed meticulousness of his person, his yard, and his home. Curtis Smith greeted me at the door, immaculate and starched in white collared shirt, khaki pants with carefully pleated front, and white tennis shoes. His hair was short and sandy; his face regular-featured and plain; his bearing military. In his retirement, Curtis had apparently taken up several hobbies, including putting large model ships into small bottles and raising tropical fish. These hobbies were all spread out meticulously in the front rooms of the house where the living room and dining room would normally be.

"Glad to meet you," he said and gave my hand a firm pump.

"Likewise," I said, striving for laconic.

"Would you like a cool drink?" he offered, betraying a southern upbringing. Who else would offer iced tea in December?

"No, thanks," I replied and handed him my card.

We sat down in the workroom with the tropical fish tank. It was enormous and stocked not only with odd-looking colorful fish, but exotic-looking, probably flesh-eating plants, to say nothing of thousands of dollars worth of oxygenating pumps, filters, and the like.

"You must be terribly concerned about your daughter," I ventured. "Do you have any idea where she might be or why?"

Curtis Smith looked sad. "I've been somewhat out of touch with Courtney and her mother since the remarriage," he said somewhat stiffly. "I don't get to see her as much as I'd like."

I sympathized; at least I thought so. But there was something secretive and forbidding about him that I couldn't quite trust.

"I knew that Montgomery would come between us. He's poison. He only married Emily for her money. That's obvious." Pause. "Of course, I was away a lot. My job took me away a lot."

"So you have no idea where Courtney might have disappeared?"

"No idea. It's a terrible family situation. I don't blame Courtney for trying to get away."

As I contemplated my next question, my eyes wandered away to neat stacks of *National Geographic*, presumably from the year ought-seven. On another shelf, I spied a carefully constructed many-tiered rack, which held what must have been hundreds of matchbook covers from around the world. Ah, the companion collection to the one in Courtney's bedroom.

As I couldn't come up with another question, I decided to leave Mr. Smith to his hobbies and his personal remorse.

"Please do call me, Mr. Smith, if you hear from Courtney," I said, and then added with some trepidation, "I have reason to believe that Courtney flew to Oaxaca, Mexico. Do you know any reason why she would have done that?"

"No idea," he said.

"If you were me," I queried, "would you try to follow her down there?"

"Depends how good your contacts are," he said.

Not having any contacts whatsoever, I sighed, thanked Mr. Smith, and let him walk me to the door. My original plan was intact. How I wished I'd paid more attention in Spanish class.

13

Passage to Oaxaca

IT WAS about 3:30 when I drove into Sibley Hospital to see if anything had changed in Will's condition. It was eerily quiet as usual in the halls as I approached the nursing station for the Intensive Care Unit.

"No change at all," said the nurse on duty.

"No sign of consciousness," repeated the resident, who had the day shift.

I was allowed into the room—Will's was one of six beds, with all manner of equipment hooked up. He was bandaged and tubed, but looked serene. Both hands were folded over the covers. I put my hand on his for a moment, afraid to disturb him. I had brought one of Will's prized pet pigs—of pink stone—and placed it on the rolling table by his bed, so that he would see something familiar if he should wake up.

I then went into the main waiting room to wait for Marna and Michael, whom I expected any minute. They arrived together in a little bit, and they each hugged me silently. They had been in to see Will a little earlier and knew about as much as I did. I filled them in on my frenetic day's work and told them that I had booked a flight from Dulles International Airport through Mexico City to Oaxaca early the next morning.

I could tell that they were reluctant to let me go on my own, but were torn by not wanting to leave Will and needing to attend to the agency's other business. I'll admit that I bristled at their lack of confidence in me. Will was clearly *pater familias* and Marna everyone's mother—but would

I always be the little kid of the family? The one everyone had to look out for? The one thought most likely to get lost or scrape her knee?

And if it were so, was it because I really was the new kid on the block or because I actually wanted to be the new kid for keeps? Did I want to be a full player, on my own, or did I want to be taken care of? Was that why I kept finding myself in dubious marriages? Because I longed for security even at the price of dependency? I took a silent vow then and there, that I would be a full player. I had assured Will Thompson in my initial interview that I was fearless, and I intended to live up to it.

Fighting Marna and Michael's solicitude, I reassured them that I would be fine in Mexico and that I would keep in constant touch. They agreed reluctantly, but Michael said that he would apply for a Tourist Card the next day just in case I needed back-up. (I had one from an earlier trip just across the border to Guadalajara. Marna didn't need one because she never flew anywhere.) Michael said that he would try to find the name of a reputable detective agency in Oaxaca and make contact, as that was the most efficient way to work in a foreign country. Above all, they warned me, I was to travel only as a tourist. I could be thrown in jail in Mexico for working a job without a work permit. I had absolutely no right to be practicing detection on their turf. The advice kept flowing fast and furious.

"Just relax, guys," I had to say finally. "Show a little confidence."

The next morning found me at Dulles International Airport, decked out in full tourist garb, camera around my neck, a small green roll-on suitcase in my hand. Without incident I boarded a nearly empty plane and had a smooth connecting flight to Mexico City. I promptly dozed off reading a guidebook to Mexico that I had picked up at Borders Books the day before.

The chapter on Oaxaca began, "Oaxaca, small, charming, and quaint. A town 340 miles south of Mexico City where the sun smiles all the year.

Situated in an immense valley but still at an altitude of better that 5,000 feet, Oaxaca is warmer than Mexico City and a little more tropical. There are many colorful Zapotec Indian markets in and around Oaxaca, nearly unchanged for hundreds of years."

On the next page, I read, "Oaxaca is a land of generous sun. The ruins surrounding the city are, archeologically, among the most interesting in the world. *Monte Alban* is one of the most important and spectacular pre-Hispanic ruins in Mexico. The enormous pyramids, tombs, temples, and ball courts are isolated on the top of a majestic mountain 10 kilometers outside the city."

"The ruins of *Mitla*," the book continued, "are located in a mostly Zapotec-speaking village, 46 kilometers due east of Oaxaca. These ruins are famous for their repeating and intricate geometric motifs, reminiscent of Greek design."

I dozed off and dreamed of pre-Colonial cities, filled with grand carved pyramids and colorful markets. Then, in the dream, I met Will, Michael, and Marna, who began cautioning me in unison not to drink the water.

I woke up with a start. I looked at my watch and realized that I barely had time to review my notes and study Courtney's picture until I had memorized every aspect of her face. Who was Courtney, anyway? I got out my stack of photos, some posed, some Polaroid candids. Her mother called her carefree; her stepfather called her "boy crazy." Her birth father thought that she was troubled by her mother's remarriage. They could all be right. Courtney's face was oddly expressionless—just shallow or hiding something? Her features were regular, her skin tanned, and her light-brown hair streaked with blond. She looked ordinary, typical, but maybe a little lost.

After five hours of air travel, I debarked into the Mexico City airport. Flustered, I looked around me for something familiar. I knew I was in a Latin country from the general air of confusion and celebration. Two dogs were racing over the checkerboard marble floor, and three little boys were playing soccer on roller skates—over and under and in-between scattered baggage and string-tied parcels.

Where was the line to the information desk, I wondered? The line to check in? The line to security? The line to anything? People stood about haphazardly, munching tortillas, smoking cigars. How was I to make the connecting flight to Oaxaca? People milled around me comfortably, laughing, gesticulating, and conspicuously displaying affection.

Finally, summoning up my best Spanish, I buttonholed a man wearing a uniform with lots of braid and asked, "Donde esta el aeroplano a Oaxaca?"

"I speak no English," he said in terror, trying to disengage himself.

Stubbornly, I hung on. "But I am speaking Spanish."

With a wrench of a button, he tore himself away and attended to other matters.

"Can I be of assistance?" said a handsome man vaguely reminiscent of Ricardo Montelban.

"Please. Do you know where to board the plane to Oaxaca?"

"Ah, Oaxaca. I love it well." Like the Spaniards in a Hemingway novel, he seemed to be translating into formal English. "Oaxaca," he warmed to his subject, "a city with a soul. Ah—if only I am artist of the painting brush—" He waved his hands in frustration.

I hated to seem mundane, but "The flight to Oaxaca?"

Somewhat condescendingly, he pointed me to the departure/arrival board, which, to be honest, was only a few feet away. I thanked him and walked up to the board. Tucked in between the flight to Aruba and one to Guatemala, I found my flight number and departure gate. This wasn't so hard. Just because I was in a foreign country, on a dubious mission, having to converse in a language that I had last studied in junior high.

I handed in my ticket and walked with the other passengers onto the runway to board a small plane, a 20-seater, I thought. Once settled into my seat, I looked sideways at my seatmate the way people do on planes.

Hmmm. Texas Ranger macho. Slim jeans, bolo tie, and boots. Everything about this fellow conjured up visions of flat lands and dull conversation. As if in response to my thoughts, he turned and looked at me appraisingly, his eyes squinty, as if used to staring across acres of nothingness, daring trouble to make a move.

I don't like that kind of look.

Fortunately, the visual standoff ended when a stewardess materialized, tall and gorgeous. She leaned over me and said to the cowboy, "Can ah get y' awl anything, sir?"

He smiled and said, "A rum and Coke would come in right handy."

Good golly, I thought. He is just too perfect. But, suggestable as I am to local specialties, the drink sounded good and I ordered one, too. Then I got out the *New York Times* crossword puzzle and ostentatiously began to work on it in ink.

Miss Junior Miss of 1983 came back with two drinks on a tray and handed the cowboy his drink, spilling quite a lot on me in the process.

"Sorry, darlin'," she said, looking at him, while handing me my rum and Coke. "I'm really sorry about that little fuss-up," she said. "Would you like another drink, sir?"

"Plenty left, honey, no harm done." The cowboy smiled broadly, deepening the squint lines around his blue eyes.

"Be good now, y'hear?" The stewardess left with a languishing backward glance.

I said nothing but made a big production of blotting my crossword puzzle with my drink coaster. The rum and Coke had run the letters together into a wavy blue soup.

"Look!" said my seatmate, suddenly gesturing with his drink toward the window and sprinkling a few more brown drops my way. "There's Popocatepetl and Ixtaccihuatl!"

I put down my drink and looked out the window too. It was awesome. I could only stare in wonder at the snow-covered peaks of the volcanoes, towering above the steep, dark slopes of the thickly wooded mountains.

For the rest of the trip, we sat silently, almost companionable, in our admiration for the scenery.

As our plane steeply descended, my seatmate half rose, put on his brown cowhide jacket and said over his shoulder, "I sure do hope you have a reservation somewhere. The Alameda Park can be awful cold at night this time of year."

"Thank you all for your concern," I said tartly, "but I'll be fine." Gosh, he was smug. I realized, of course, that I had no reservations at all. But how difficult could it be to find one room in a middle-sized tourist city?

I deboarded quickly. Oaxaca airport was a one-building affair, with two very flat runways on a huge plain, surrounded by some of the most beautiful mountains I had seen since the Rockies. I wheeled my small green tote bag to a short line through customs and was just about to enter into negotiations with a taxi driver when the cowboy dude, my seatmate, drove up in a beaten-up brown Ford pick-up and offered me a ride to my hotel. I was more grateful than proud, and I thanked him.

"Are you a tourist, a native, or an expatriate?" I asked. My curiosity was getting the better of me.

"None of the above," he said curtly. "Where can I drop you?"

I thought quickly and decided that, since in fact I had no reservation at any hotel and actually didn't even know the name of any hotel, I had better try something else. I concluded that the better part of valor was to ask to be dropped off at the police station.

He looked at me questioningly.

"I'm looking for a missing friend," I said.

"Okay," he said noncommittally. "How good is your Spanish?"

"Not good," I admitted. I tried to calculate the years since junior high but it was too discouraging.

"Well, then, I'll help you make a few inquiries."

This man had to be a native. He drove right to the police station on the north outskirts of town. This wasn't the picturesque quarter, I could tell. It had stone and cement apartments, the hospital, and a small police station and lock-up. It looked like the stereotype of a Mexican police station, the kind where you didn't want to get sent for being caught in possession of an illegal substance.

My new friend, the dude, asked me my name and told me that he was Archie Hayes. He asked me the name of my missing friend and I told him Courtney Smith. Then we went up to the sergeant sitting at the desk, engrossed in a paperback novel and absent-mindedly chewing on some sticky-looking sweets.

"Si?" he said, looking up.

Archie asked to see the chief detective (Hmm, was Archie a regular here?) and the sergeant left his post briefly. A few minutes later we were ushered into a private office. I shook hands with a Detective Mestas and introduced myself. Archie told him in rapid Spanish that I was looking for a friend named Courtney Smith, an American girl, who had disappeared in Oaxaca some days ago.

"And why do you want to find this girl?" said Detective Mestas in near-perfect English.

"Uh, no reason in particular," I said. I remembered the oft-repeated strict warnings about never admitting to working in Mexico without a work permit. The police were unfriendly to freelance private investigators the world over, and that went double in Mexico. One was a tourist first, last, and only. "It's just that I was supposed to meet Courtney here and I seem to have lost track of her. She didn't call to tell me where she was staying."

He looked scornful at this lame-sounding explanation but replied politely nonetheless. "It is usually very hard to find an American in Oaxaca at this time of year. However, in this case I can give you at least a little help. It so happens that I am looking for her, too."

Shock and fear come over me. The Mexican police wanted Courtney?

"Well, I don't know yet how worrisome this is, but today I was called by (he consulted a notebook) a Señor Mario Bueno, the proprietor of the Hotel Casa Paradiso on the street Heroes de Chapultepec. He told me that an American girl of that name had registered at his hotel four days ago, and had disappeared two days later, leaving her belongings and failing to pay her bill. His interest is, of course, financial. Mine is the suspicion of foul play.

"We are very much concerned that Oaxaca remain the picturesque and safe tourist haven that it has been over the years. As you know, the Christmas season is our busiest, culminating in the Procession of the Radishes. Of course, we have many police deployed through the city, but we are not unaware that there are unscrupulous people about preying on tourists, picking their pockets and such. There are also at least two gueril-la groups in our areas—The National Liberation Army, which operates mostly in the Southern State of Chiapas, as well as the Popular Revolutionary Army, the second largest rebel group, which has attacked as close to us as Acapulco. Nine people were killed. I cannot tell you whether your friend has simply skipped town or met with some trouble, but we are eager to know. Do you have a photograph of the missing girl?"

I handed over one of my many photos. Detective Mestas handed me his card, and we promised to keep in touch.

"And what will you do now?" he inquired.

"Well, I need a hotel anyway, so I think that I'll try to get a room at the Hotel Casa Paradiso and hope Courtney comes back." (Quick think-ing, I congratulated myself. Just what a tourist would do.)

I thanked Inspector Mestas, and Archie and I walked out. Archie again volunteered to drop me off, and again I accepted, hating to be in the debt of this helpful cowboy, but needing the lift. Archie dropped me off at the hotel, closer into the town, but still on the north side.

"Good luck, my gringa friend," he said and tipped his hat good-bye.

14

Hotel Casa Paradiso

THE HOTEL CASA PARADISO did not live up to the grandeur of its name. Calling this small structure a "hotel" was stretching it a bit, and yet it didn't have the homey feel of a "casa." It looked like a sort of down-at-the-heels boarding house. By no stretch of the imagination did it conjure up Paradise. It looked reasonably nice, though, nestled on a broad tree-shaded street not far from the public library in a residential neighborhood.

Mostly, I felt extraordinarily lucky to have gotten such a great lead on Courtney. Twenty-four hours ago she could have been anywhere in the world. Now I was standing exactly where she had been 48 hours ago. It was true that she could once again be anywhere in the world, but I tried to see the glass half-full, not half-empty—to see the Tequila bottle and not the worm in it—was my new motto. The answer that I was not nearer to, however, was why Courtney had been here. If I knew that I might be closer to finding her.

I went inside to the front desk and the plump, balding hotel manager, Mario Bueno, was more than friendly. He assured me that he had one room available. Thank heavens, his English was excellent, in addition to being idiosyncratic and spirited. He told me, when I complimented him, that he had learned his English in England, and warned me that any difficulties in my understanding his pronunciation could be attributed to his British accent. He had been a waiter at the Savoy Hotel in London for six months and occasionally enlivened his conversation with "tip tops" and "jolly wells."

The amenities over, Mr. Bueno became business-like. "Por favor, sign here. Under the line." Mario presented the hotel register and handed me a ballpoint pen. I read the headings: *Nombre* or *Name* was easy. For *Profession,* I put tourist. The process was easy until I came to the last category: *Destino*. Ah, if I only knew....

"Señor Bueno," I began after completing the form and handing over my Tourist Card for inspection, "I am looking for my young American friend, Courtney Smith. She should have already checked in here, but I haven't heard from her. Do you know where I can find her?"

His manner descended at once to the very chilly as he explained that she had left the Hotel Casa Paradiso suddenly without paying her bill. "The police have been informed," he added ominously.

I quickly took out my wallet and insisted on paying my friend's bill. "Did she leave anything behind?" I asked innocently. "Perhaps later I could look at her room and keep her things with me till she gets back."

"Jolly good," said Mario in his more typical friendly manner. "Why don't you get settled in first?" I would have asked to have looked immediately, but didn't want to seem too eager. "Rodriguez!" Mario used his hands as a megaphone and bellowed again. "Rodriguez!"

From behind the cigarette machine a young man slowly emerged and somewhat reluctantly picked up my bag. He was, like his American counterparts, attached to a Walkman and evidently marching to a different drummer. At odd times, he would snap his fingers at rhythmic patterns heard only by him. I followed his dark leather jacket with many zippers through a courtyard, sparsely decorated with a few mariposa lilies and one lone banyan tree.

"Up-estairs," he said, turning around briefly. And up we went to the second floor. "Aqui," he said, and dropped my luggage on the floor. I handed him the pesos in my pocket, promising myself that I would familiarize myself with the currency, and he went off, still in the universal teenage world of rock.

My room was decent enough, at least by daylight. Oh, whom was I kidding? It was small, stuffy, with green wallpaper, and a linoleum floor. Frankly, there was something pretty depressing about it. It was the sort of place where if you died alone in the night, no one would find you for days. It was the kind of a place where you could lose your will to go on and simply take to your bed like a Henry James character, finally turning your face to the wall. But I resolutely settled in, and in the dim room, the shutters of the window on the courtyard closed against the afternoon sun, I was soon partaking of an unanticipated nap.

Sometime later I woke up in the semi-darkness and groped for the light. It wasn't where it ought to have been on the table beside my bed, and as my eyes became accustomed to the gloom, I saw a faint glimmer through the window to an unfamiliar courtyard. I roused myself and got out of bed, putting my feet on some cold but sticky linoleum, took two steps, and reached up for the pull cord on the ceiling light.

I knew where I was. A hotel room in Oaxaca, Mexico. The room was papered with limegreen plastic, stamped with the shapes of olive unconvincing green roses. The floor was darkgreen squares. An unidentified crawling object scuttled past. The room had a bed, a dresser, a closet, and attached bathroom that I dared not enter. "Hotel Casa Paradiso"—not.

I looked at my watch with the lighted dial and found that it was only 7:00 p.m. I was sitting on my lumpy bed, staring at dust balls and thinking I was only suspicious of dirt that moved, when there was a knock on my door and almost simultaneously, the person who knocked walked briskly in.

It was an American woman, birdlike, and small, in her mid-fifties, I would guess. She was wearing a polyester pantsuit in tan and some Mexican silver bracelets.

"Hello," she said with authority. "I'm Marjorie Daws, your next-door neighbor."

Energetically, she inspected my room, picking up and putting down my toiletries and studying my other belongings as she talked. I was too stunned to complain.

"How did you find the hotel?" she interrogated. "Are you in Mexico for a vacation?"

"Yes, I came down for fun, and—" I smiled half-heartedly.

"Oh?" Marjorie picked up my bottle of Pepto-Bismol. "You'll need the larger size." She put it down.

I began to feel as if I were remiss in my duties as hostess. I half-rose from the bed and made a vague gesture around me. "I'm Schaeffer Brown. Won't you sit down?"

There was no place to light. I was sitting on my cot-like bed and the one chair was piled high with the contents of my bag.

"Sit?" Marjorie looked around. "Can't do it. I'm not a tourist," she said with the pride of the native speaking to the interloper. "I work here. I live in Oaxaca all year round." She picked up and read the directions on my can of bug spray and laughed bitterly as she put it down. "The size of the insects you find here"—she spread her hands a good two feet "thrive on that sort of thing." She pointed to the can. "It's vitamins for them." She came closer and said menacingly, "To say nothing of the lizards—iguanas. Some morning you'll get up and find one in your shoe."

I instinctively lifted my feet from the floor and tucked them under me.

"Yes," I said, feeling as if I had lost my place in the script. "Fun and relaxation. That's what I was looking forward to. This hotel seems to be just the place to find it."

"Although—"

I leaned forward. "You were saying, Marjorie," I prompted. "'Although'?"

"Although?" She looked at me, puzzled. "Oh yes, I was just thinking that it's been a little hectic here this past week."

"Hectic?" I looked out the window at the lone banyan tree swaying in the courtyard. "It seems rather low-key to me."

"Last week," Marjorie came nearer to me, looked around to make sure no one was listening, and then, as a further precaution, lowered her voice. "Last week we had an incident."

"An incident?"

"Yes, a young American girl who was staying here suddenly disappeared, leaving all her belongings," she finished dramatically.

A young American girl. "Had she been here long?"

"No, she had just gotten here—a few days before. She was a strange girl. Aimless. She didn't seem to have any interests." Marjorie coughed. "Except men. She was interested in men."

"Did she have regular features and long, brown hair with blond streaks?"

"Yes." Marjorie wrinkled her brow.

"A light tan and a blank expression?" I pulled out one of my many photos—she looked puzzled.

"I guess that's her."

"She's a friend of mine," I explained. "I was supposed to meet her here. Do you have any idea where she went?"

Suddenly Marjorie clammed up. "You had better talk to Mario about that. He knows more about it than I do."

Just then there was another knock on the door. What was this? Grand Central Station? A slightly older man enclosed in a very stiff Mexican blanket resembling a giant sandwich board edged in. Under it could be discerned black nylon socks and brown huaraches. He smelled a bit musty. Perhaps with the tang of day-old tamales and moldy newspapers. When he smiled, he showed large yellow teeth.

"Greetings and felicitations to the new arrival." He bowed and the fringes of his blanket knocked over my camera. The new arrival stared at me intently. Behind his glasses, held up on one side by a tan rubber band, his brown eyes were probing. I was a source of great interest. Like shipwrecked sailors stranded on an island, the regulars were clearly parched for novelty.

"Hello, Professor Hudson," said Marjorie, glad of the interruption. "I was just leaving, but meet Miss—"

"Brown," I said, "Schaeffer Brown."

"Another North American tourist," Marjorie explained unnecessarily.

"Ah, and have you been telling her the latest gossip?"

"I don't know what you mean," Marjorie said primly.

"About Courtney Smith, of course."

"I think that was her name," said Marjorie, edging toward the door. "I really didn't know her very well."

"The poor little Magdalena—she seemed to be"—he paused and leered—"at loose ends. She had—how you say?—transient male companions. Of course, I don't like to repeat gossip," he paused and held out his arms, "but what else can you do with it?"

"Did you know Courtney well, Professor Hudson?" I asked.

"Not well at all. She stayed so briefly. Besides, she seemed to consider me *hors de combat* in the field of love." He laughed and then stopped abruptly and tried to sound more solemn. "Of course, her disappearance was upsetting." He bowed his head in a moment of silence. "Don't misunderstand me. Nobody is more upset than I am over her untimely exit from our little stage. 'Bent is the branch that should have grown full straight,' '*De mortuis*,' and all that sort of thing. But," he lowered his voice, "there was something strange about that girl. Something—" I handed him the photo. "Yes, that is the young vagabond."

Marjorie cut him short. "I really must go." She held out her hand gingerly, like the Dean's wife at a faculty party, and said grimly, "I hope you have a pleasant stay."

After her departure, Professor Hudson made himself at home. He placed all the contents on my chair onto my bureau dresser and lowered himself carefully into the chair. He was right to do so because it was the rickety kind that has to have a small piece of paper under one of the legs for balance.

"I'm sure Marjorie had more pressing duties—perhaps keeping up her Dwight D. Eisenhower scrapbook," he smiled wickedly. "But let me introduce myself—Kyley Hudson, Professor Emeritus, and your neighbor." And he got up and bowed. "I don't actually live in the hotel, of course, but in my van parked next door to it. I carry my house on my back like a turtle."

"I think, Professor," I wanted to return to the subject, "that I really need to look for Courtney Smith, now. I was supposed to meet her here. I need to see her things, her room, talk to the manager...."

"So sorry, dear girl, but I really have no further information, and everything is locked up tight for the night here at the hotel. The Casa does not offer twenty-four-hour-a-day service. You have to beg on bended knee to get a small libation or a piece of frayed towel. I'm afraid you'll have to wait for morning to make your inquiries." He peered more closely at me.

"Perhaps you'd like to come to my van and share a cup of chamomile tea—and very, very boiled water."

"Thank you, no. I've had a long trip and I'm tired." I pantomimed a large yawn.

The Professor got up. "Then I wish you pleasant dreams and goodnight." He was halfway out the door when he turned his head and said, "Perhaps a conversation with Rosa Calderon, our handmaiden, will prove fruitful."

"Where can I find her?"

"Don't worry, my young friend, she'll find you." And drawing the fuzzy folds of his reboza about him, he was gone.

15

The Woman in White

AFTER THE PROFESSOR'S DEPARTURE, and a decent interval, I walked downstairs to use the office telephone. Mario was at his post behind the desk, watching what appeared to be an episode of *Dallas* in Spanish. I asked him if he could help me make a call to the U.S.; he showed me how, and I dialed the office number.

Marna picked up, with a chipper "Will Thompson Agency. Can I help you?"

"Marna, it's Schaeffer. I'm in Oaxaca, Mexico," I said and gave her the name and the phone number of the hotel. "I have some leads on Courtney, but haven't found her yet." Then I asked about Will.

"I'm afraid he's no better, dear," Marna said soothingly. "But then no worse either. 'Serious but stable' is what the hospital says. He hasn't really come to yet."

"Oh," I said dejectedly. "Marna, any idea of who did this to Will? Was it someone he helped put away back in the old days, an angry husband? What?"

"The police have no leads, they said. No witnesses except you and Will. Michael and I have been over the crime scene again and again, but we've found nothing. They sent the bullet to be analyzed, of course, but we won't hear for a few days. And Michael and I have got to keep the other cases moving...."

"Of course, Marna, The agency means everything to Will. I know that you're doing whatever you can."

"Do you need any help down there, Schaeffer?"

"Not at all," I said firmly. "It still may be an innocent disappearance, but there are other possibilities as well. There is crime and political terrorism in this part of Mexico, so I need to move quickly. Can you call Mrs. Crawford and tell her that I'm hot on the trail—and see if she can think of anything else I should know? And if you would, could you also call Courtney's father, Curtis, and her stepfather, Montgomery? See if they've heard anything."

Then I asked to speak with Michael. I didn't have anything particular to say, but I just missed him and wanted to hear his voice. Marna told me that he wasn't in. I thought about telling Marna about how Mexico seemed strange for all its colorful people. How I felt alone in a world of transients. How I despaired of ever finding Courtney. But I remembered my vow to myself to be stronger. Besides, Marna had bravely forged on as a widow for the last 20 years.

"Marna," I said instead, "A cowboy dude who was sitting next to me on the plane spilled a rum and Coke all over my Sunday puzzle."

"Never mind, dear. It was too easy for you anyway. Michael and I have gone on to the Puns and Anagrams in the *Times Literary Supplement* anyway. Much more challenging. We'll show you when you get back. Now, keep in touch."

That night after talking with Marna, I ate the package of crackers and the apple I had saved from the flight, and then I couldn't think of anything to do but try to get back to sleep. I read in my guidebook a little, but I couldn't seem to drift off. It was too hot, then too cold. I tried to conjugate some Spanish verbs but that didn't do the trick. I got up to turn on the overhead bulb and attempted a trip to the bathroom. I went to the door and turned on the light switch. A very large insect, transfixed by the light, stopped in its tracks. It looked like some terrible hybrid from a sci-fi movie, perhaps a throwback to the Pleistocene period, now come back ready to inherit the earth.

We both stood there motionless. I held my breath. I knew that I was bigger than it was and that he was more afraid of me than I was of him. But did I have 26 legs, who knows how many poison-laden tentacles, and a general tendency to dart up a person's pants?

I refused to give up the battlefield to the cucaracha for both philosophical and practical reasons. I turned out the bathroom light and temporarily retreated to get the bug spray. When I got back to the bathroom, the insectus giganticus had outsmarted me and had disappeared.

After using the bathroom, I paced up and down my room, my incipient claustrophobia starting to kick in. I had never been so wide-awake in my life. I measured off the area, nine by eleven-and-a-half. Then I looked at the one adornment on the wall—an improbably orange sunset over Lake Titicaca. Next I read the hotel rates printed on the back of the door—they were only some 200 pesos lower than the price I had agreed to pay.

After a while, this perfectly ordinary cheaply priced hotel room was beginning to feel like a narrow, pest-ridden box. I could smell DDT under a sickeningly sweet cover.

I clearly needed more air. I walked to the window, pulled at the blind, which went up with a zip, and opened the window. The air was balmy and the courtyard lovely and peaceful. I took several deep cleansing breaths and felt much better.

And then I saw it, her—whatever. A slim woman's figure with long brown hair and a long white Mexican dress. "Courtney," I called out. "Courtney." I ran out of my room and down the stairs, past the now-quiet front desk and out to the courtyard. By the time I got there, the figure had vanished.

Could it really have been Courtney? Or had weariness and jet lag caused me to hallucinate?

16

Rosa Calderon

"I HAVE wakened you, Señora?"

In the doorway, a slim and attractive Mexican woman with dark eyes, assertive brows, a straight nose, and lovely full lips was speaking to me. Her long glossy brown hair was tied back into a low ponytail, and she was wearing a white buttoned-down shirtdress that seemed to signify "housekeeper."

"Hello," I said, struggling to become alert. "My name is Schaeffer Brown." I yawned and propped myself up on my elbows. "Could you please tell me what time it is?"

"Eight o'clock. I have twelve rooms to do this morning. And you are my second person. Room 102," she offered as explanation, a little sullenly.

"Are you Señorita Rosa Calderon?"

"Yes. Rosa Calderon. You have heard of me then?"

"Well, Professor Hudson mentioned you."

I wanted to ask about Courtney, but I thought it might be more productive to lead up to it gradually. "Señorita Rosa, I wonder..." I moved uneasily under the blanket as I remembered my midnight encounter with the bug from outer space. "Last night I found something hovering in the bathroom."

"What was it?" she asked somewhat impatiently. "Show me."

I got out of bed and led her to the bathroom. "Here." I pointed to the brownish tile. "Last night I saw something very large creeping around."

Rosa bent down and looked fixedly at the floor. "I see nothing."

I got down on my hands and knees and looked. Nothing. If there's anything worse than a large bug that is there, it's a large bug that isn't there but is lurking in the drain or under the soap, smiling and getting ready to strike as soon as it gets you alone.

"But Marjorie," I coughed apologetically as I tried to get back my credibility, "I met her last night and she said—"

"Oh, her. Señora Marjorie." She snorted and then she hit her left elbow with her right hand. "Tacana. I think you call it 'stingy.' Never buy anything herself. Don't cry me about Señora Marjorie." Rosa dismissed the whole subject and left the bathroom. She started a strenuous feather-dusting of the room, humming under her breath.

I followed her. "Señorita Rosa?" She just hummed more loudly. There seemed no way to get back what there was of our rapport, so I decided to plunge right in. "Señora Marjorie—I mean someone—suggested that you might know something about the young American girl who disappeared from the hotel." I showed her the photos. She nodded in recognition.

"Disappeared!" Rosa put down the feather duster and crossed herself. "No. She was chased away."

"Chased?" Here was the possibility of another scenario. "You think she was chased away?" I sat down on the edge of my bed. "How do you know?"

"I know."

"But who chased her?"

"La Llorona."

"La Llorona? Who's that?"

"La Llorona is a seducer of men, a killer of women."

"Why don't they catch her and put her in prison?"

Rosa laughed at my naivete. "They can't catch her. You can't even see her hardly ever." She bent over the bed and looked directly into my eyes. "You can only hear her in the night, crying for her lost children. She goes about like the air."

"What happened to—to La Llorona?" I was beginning to feel doubtful about the whole story.

"What happened? I tell you what happened." Rosa sat down on the side of the bed. "La Llorona had many children, but her lover left her and she go loca—crazy. She drowned her children in a river and now, now every night she goes out and looks for them."

"But what does all this have to do with Courtney?"

"Wait, I tell you." Rosa didn't like being interrupted. "La Llorona goes out at night to get the men to love her and then she kills them. But sometime she kills the women who take the men away from their sweethearts—the bad women."

"What does La Llorona look like?"

"God does not let all people see her. But I can see her. She looks like a beautiful woman. She has long hair and her dress is blanco. I can see her."

"When? When do you see her?" I was beginning to be infected with her certitude.

"Every night."

"But why would La Llorona want to hurt Courtney?"

"Ai." Rosa made a gesture of contempt. "Your American Courtney no inocente. She go with many men." She paused and looked down. "She go with my man."

"Your man?"

"Yes, my man. El Coyote. I loved him." She put her hands on her heart and her eyes filled with tears. " He was not only my lover, but my teacher. He was teaching me that this—" she looked around her "—is not all there is in life. That this—" she held up her feather duster "—is not all that I can do."

To Rosa's dismay, tears began to brim over. She pushed them away with impatience. "When I find out that Coyote has another woman, I beg him, 'Ah, mi amor, mi vida, come back to me.'"

"Did he come back?"

"No, he was bewitched." Rosa shook her head mournfully.

I couldn't believe that Courtney would be such a temptress. From what I knew of her, she didn't seem to have the energy for it. But her stepfather, Montgomery, had told me that she was wild and boy-crazy.

Rosa grabbed my arm. "I cry to him, 'Coyote, even if you have una enamorada, come back to me.' Your American friend was not the first time," she said softly with something like shame. I felt for her, remembering my own men who had strayed. Perhaps I didn't love them as much as Rosa loved El Coyote, but I felt the loss and the betrayal.

Just then a face materialized at the half-open door of my room. It was the manager, Mario Bueno.

"Rosa, they want you in Room 101. They say the room is not in tiptop condition."

Rosa flashed me an angry look and picked up her feather duster.

"Wait! Señorita Rosa!" I said. "Do you know where Courtney is now?"

"No, Señora." Her face hardened.

"Is La Llorona real? Or just a myth, a story?"

"She is real and a myth," Rosa said thoughtfully. "You know, I have gone to Catholic School. I want to continue my education and become a teacher here in Oaxaca. I do not want to be a housekeeper cleaning tourists' rooms for my whole life. But I am also an Indian. A Zapotec. My family lives in the town of Teotitlan. I can go there, too, and be at home."

"Rosa!" Mario called more sharply this time.

"Caramba!" Rosa muttered and strode out of the room, closing the door behind her.

Moments later I heard a knock on my door. It was Mario Bueno wanting to come in and speak to me. I began to feel like Madame Pompadour entertaining in bed at a levee at Versailles. I got under the covers and pulled the sheet up.

"Señor Mario," I called through the door, "could you wait one moment downstairs? I want to ask you something, too." I quickly slipped into a sundress and sandals and visited the bathroom cautiously. Then I went down to see Mario.

"Dios Mio," he said, when I showed Mario Courtney's picture just to be sure that we were talking about the same girl who had absconded without paying. Mario coughed apologetically. "I'm sorry, Señorita, but all gringas look alike to me. The old ones wear flowered shirts with a camera around their neck, and the young ones wear blue jeans and tennis shoes and carry a pack on their back."

"Señor Mario. This is the young woman that I was supposed to meet. May I please see her room?"

"Sorry," he said, sounding relieved. "After the police came, we cleaned up the room. And then the people from the library came and took everything there is. It is very sad."

"The library?"

"Yes, right down the street. They keep things for their jumble sales to support the library."

"Well, can you point me to the library? Is it open now?"

"Yes, yes. It is open all of the time. It is right down the street. You must turn left when you leave the hotel."

"Thanks, thanks very much." I said, and turned to leave with what he must have felt to be Yankee brusqueness. But he seemed relieved to see me go.

"De nada, Senorita." He waved his hand in farewell. "Hasta la vista."

The library was more prepossessing than the Hotel Casa Paradiso—at least on the outside. It was housed in a model of Spanish Colonial architecture, with a stone facade and an elaborately carved portal. I went in under the graceful colonnades and approached a series of courtyards. In the center of the innermost courtyard was a fountain surrounded by green foliage and red flowers. But inside was another story. I pushed open a huge wooden door and all was instant gloom. It took a minute or so to adjust my eyes to the darkness. With difficulty I made out two small rooms and stacks of books. I went over to the nearest shelf to look at the offerings before I went about asking my questions.

Although the volumes were organized strictly according to the latest rulings of the Library of Congress, the books themselves were a pitiful conglomeration. They looked like a collection you would find in the floating library of the Queen Elizabeth II—everybody's rejects with the careful bookplate on the frontispiece, e.g., "Donated by Richard Mosely, February 1956." The titles were what you would expect: *Darkness at Noon* by Arthur Koestler (donated by E. Edward Grisholm, February 1965); *Girl of the Limberlost* by Gene Stratton Porter; *Fascinating History of Numerology and What it Can Do for You*; two copies of a Vanity Press edition of *Meditations* by Alice R. Claghorn; a beautifully bound hardcover edition of *The Yale Class of 1949 Yearbook*; and, finally, many dog-eared copies of murder mystery paperbacks.

Holding a copy of Alice R. Claghorn's *Meditations* in my hand to show sincerity, I groped my way to the desk and discerned a proto-librarian sitting there, checking her files. Boston-patrician, quietly disapproving, horn-rimmed glasses, high-necked brown dress, she was every librarian who has ever terrorized you since sixth grade.

I edged closer. When I got directly in front of this archetype, I gasped. It was Marjorie Daws, my Hotel Casa Paradiso next-door neighbor. But a Marjorie who had morphed into a librarian. Now she sat upright in her chair, controlled and corseted. Her navy-blue dress was fastened so securely at the neck that she looked like she would choke. If she loosened her collar, I was sure her neck would go swoosh—like an opened coffee can.

"It's you, Marjorie. I didn't know you were the librarian."

She looked up, her brow wrinkled, staring at me over the rims of her glasses. "Yes, I help out here." Even her diction seemed more precise now. She put her hand to her hair and adjusted the pencil stuck in her bun.

"I'm sure we'll be glad to serve you to the best of our capability. And if there's anything you need from the Puebla library, perhaps my staff will be able to get it for you."

"Thank you. Thank you very much." I hesitated. "There *is* one thing. That friend of mine who came down here—the young student. Courtney Smith. Did she ever come to the library?"

"Courtney Smith?" She put her pencil to her mouth and thought. "No, I don't think so."

"Can you tell me anything more about her time here? Whom she knew? What she did in Oaxaca? Can you show me her things that were donated to the library?"

There was a silent pause. She was still chewing her pencil when a second librarian appeared behind the desk.

"Señorita—mucho gusto conocer la. My name is Ramon Gonzalez. Delighted to know you." A tall, very handsome man smiled at me. "Welcome to Oaxaca. I heard that you are wondering about the pobrecita Courtney who disappeared?"

As I have stated earlier, macho was not my type. But I had to make an exception for Ramon Gonzalez. He was macho but beautiful: radiant bronze skin, large dark eyes, lustrous black hair, and a totally engaging smile.

"I'm glad to meet you, too," I said. "My name's Schaeffer Brown and I'm a friend of Courtney's. I know that she stayed for two nights at the Hotel Casa Paradiso and that she disappeared suddenly and that the library took her things. I'm worried about her, and I'm trying to find out where she is—to reconstruct her two days before she vanished—so I wonder if you have any of her letters, her clothes—"

He looked at Marjorie. She looked at him. Was there a flicker of something between them?

Finally she said, "There really wasn't a thing. I remember thinking—how pitiful it is that she left so little behind her. But excuse me—I have work to do." And with a nod at me, she walked briskly to the reading room.

Alone with me, Ramon looked thoughtful and said, "Unfortunately our life is not like an algebra book with problems in the front pages and the clear-cut answers in back." Then Ramon smiled a dazzling white smile and said, "Come, let us walk in the garden—it's not moldy and dusty like this room"—he wrinkled his nose—"but young and fresh and beautiful like you, Señorita." He bowed and took my arm. I loathed this Latin Romantic nonsense. Truly. But he was perhaps my only lead.

Beside him, I walked out the door into the patio. He was right. Everything was green and lush, and I seemed to hear a bird singing in a tree. But now Ramon pressed my arm. "Have you ever been to Monte Alban—our greatest Zapotec ruin?"

"No." I was noncommittal. This was a business, not a pleasure trip.

"I'm taking a group up there this afternoon—I'm a guide part-time when I'm not working at the library. If you can make it, you can join our group, which will meet at Monte Alban. And I can think of anything more I can remember about Courtney."

"Thank you. I'd like to."

"Good," he said. "About three, after the siesta." He thought a minute. "You can get a bus at the Hotel Universe."

"Where's that?"

"It's easy to get to. Just walk down the hill. It's on the other side of the Zocalo." And then he clasped my arm warmly and left.

Had I been a lesser person, or a great deal less cynical one, I might have been seduced by this act. The warmth of Ramon's hand lingered on my arm. His charm had been so real I expected to see a mark. But this was business only. Ramon might know something that I needed to know and he seemed to be the only one talking just now. The clock was running. The more time that passed without Courtney's turning up, the more I felt Courtney to be in profound danger, or even, if I could dare think it, dead.

17

The Zocalo

I HEARD THE ZOCALO, the central plaza of Oaxaca, before I saw it. It was a large open square surrounded by open-air cafes and shops bustling with activity. Overhanging three sides, providing shade and charm, were stone arches. And under these arches people laughed, talked, strolled, flirted, and ate.

I stared, made almost dizzy by the different sights, sounds, and smells. American tourists brushed against Indian farmers. Mexican businessmen elbowed French hippies. Many of the travelers had tried to brighten up their outfits with bits of Mexicana. Rebozos and huipiles covered Guess jeans, and long silver earrings dangled and got caught in camera straps hung around the neck.

The native-born Mexicans were similarly eclectic in their choice of clothing. A youth wore a sombrero, carried a serape draped over his left shoulder, and stalked panther-like in Adidas sneakers. A Mexican woman, her long black hair braided with red ribbons, a serape tied around the waist of her long skirt, carried a small girl dressed in a purple nylon sweat suit.

In the center of the Plaza, a little park glistened with trees and fountains. It seemed to follow the Mexican rule—more is good, too much is better. In honor of Christmas the fir trees were completely covered with gold and silver tinsel and red, green, and blue balls. Four different fountains spouted colored water, and in front of a large creche were gaily-wrapped boxes. Near the creche, two photographers were standing beside their upright cameras, waiting patiently, while a third was posing a satisfied client, a little boy provided with a large sombrero, sitting on a painted wooden horse.

But the main attraction of the park was a dollhouse-pretty white bandstand with musicians just now playing the matador's march from *Carmen*. Surrounding the bandstand, dotted here and there, were ornate white iron benches, the resting place for many of the Mexicans from small towns who had come into the city to sell their wares and to buy provisions in return. The benches were also places of refuge for perspiring tourists, unused to the rigors of the heat, of sightseeing, and of tamales. I saw them sitting down—riffling the pages of guidebooks, loosening their belts, easing out of their shoes.

I smelled popcorn and cooking oil. Everyone was munching on something. Young and old were snacking—peanuts, pink cotton candy, maple-flavored sugar, frosted cakes, sugar cane, roasted squash seeds, fruits candied or fresh, water ices on sticks, tacos. And if they weren't eating, they were drinking—Coca-Cola, fruit ades, coconut or papaya juice. Never had I seen a population so passionate for sweets, tidbits, and soft drinks. Refreshment stands were everywhere.

Watching everyone sip, chew, and swallow made me feel thirsty and hungry. I hesitated—wondering which appetite to indulge—when I saw Marjorie, sitting at a small outdoor cafe. It was hard to miss her. Her little body sat erect against the iron back of the ice-cream parlor chair.

Now she was once again wearing her native uniform—polyester slacks plus a huipil, a Mexican vest. Beside her at the table sat the Professor, drinking a small coffee.

"I didn't know you were coming down here," I said, sitting down in a chair beside Marjorie. "We could have come together."

"Oh, hello." She seemed less than eager to see me. "This is my siesta. I'm sitting here watching the world go by."

The Professor, however, gave me a smile and said, "Welcome to my office."

"Office?"

"Yes, I sit here every day, having a small coffee, playing chess, greeting the regulars and the transients. I have regular office hours and everyone knows me."

Encouraged by his friendliness, I said, "How about your both having lunch with me at one of these restaurants?"

"Eat at one of these restaurants? Me?" Marjorie couldn't have been more horrified if I had suggested the town horse trough. "I never eat here. I only consume the boiled white meat of chicken, Nabisco Milk crackers, and bottled Spring Valley water."

"And how long have you been living here in Oaxaca?"

"Six years." She raised her chin proudly. "And I've never had the 'tourista.'"

"But I'll bet you've got a borderline case of scurvy. All those years with no green vegetables or fresh fruits."

Marjorie angrily turned her head away, but the Professor chuckled and said, "Have you ever noticed how one's eating habits reveal one's personality? Marjorie here will only ingest the purified, the fumigated, and the hermetically sealed. But our young friends like Courtney subsist entirely on junk food. Greasy salted things, candy, pizzas, Fritos, and polysorbate-flavored orange drink. And as for the Indians," here he pointed at the passersby, "no wonder they are continually masticating. It satisfies their need for something enjoyable. Even the very poor can afford a slice of pineapple. These small treats help make their hard existence bearable."

"What about your eating habits, Professor?"

"Waiter," he called out, "another cup of Sanka, por favor." He sighed. "The last year I have become abstemious—in everything. But before my most recent liver episode, I drank tequila. Rather frequently. As a matter of fact, it so mortified my insides that my daily breakfast became a puke and a Pepsi." The waiter placed a small cup in front of him. The Professor gazed at it sadly. "Ah me, the vices I have given up."

I wanted to change the subject to get back to Courtney and her activities. "By the way, Marjorie," I turned to her. "Ramon seems an interesting young man."

"Ramon," corrected Marjorie, "is brilliant, a genius with an I.Q. of two forty-nine. He ran off the charts. He's a guide, but only to the very highest echelons. When ex-President Ford visited Oaxaca, it was Ramon who took him to visit the Mitla ruins."

The Professor laughed. "And perhaps should have left him there."

Marjorie got up, glared at the Professor and said, "I can't fritter my time away here. I still have to do the filing of last month's *Newsweeks.*" She curtly nodded farewell and walked away.

The Professor looked after her little figure with an amused expression. "But really Marjorie is right. In spite of the fact that Ramon has the handicap of having graduated from the University of Oaxaca, he's quite remarkable. Marjorie lives to fuss over him and makes sure he goes to the dentist twice a year, darns his socks and sews on his buttons. Ramon is not wanting for other female companionship either."

"Just a minute, Professor." I hurriedly got up from my seat. "I think I see someone I know." And I ran after a Courtney-like figure in a red tee shirt, walking with a short stout woman. As I got nearer, the girl stopped to look at a display of black pottery. "Muy hermosa, no, Mama?" she said. And when she turned, I saw that she had olive skin and expressive dark eyebrows.

Disappointed, I walked back to the table and sat down. "Just a case of mistaken identity. But what about you, Professor? What brought you to Oaxaca?"

"Ah, mine is a sad but short tale. I am actually a professor only by courtesy. You see, I was head bartender of the Princeton Faculty Club for twenty years, and I imbibed knowledge at the same time as my teachers imbibed scotch." He looked sad and then, "But what grand larks we did have. And to what flights of fancy did my liquid concoctions inspire them. I remember an invention of mine—one quarter gin, one quarter brandy, a pinch of lemon juice—" he suddenly clapped his hands. "I know. I'll have the waiter here bring you one of my inventions. Mozo! Mozo!" He gave a loud whistle through his teeth, and a waiter came running.

"Mozo, make this young lady a 'Oaxacan Wow-wow.'"

The waiter smiled. "Si, si, one 'Wow-wow' coming up."

"No, no, please," I said. "Just coffee. But tell me," I changed the subject quickly. "How did you get to learn so much?"

"Ah," he mused, smiling. "A self-educated man is a true scholar. Besides, my bar customers used to give me little quizzes. I'll never forget old Wally Sundstrom—he was head of the English Department—giving me my Final in Shakespeare 230 after a rather prolonged drinking session." He put his head on one side. "I remember the question that really earned me an A was my succinct comparison of the characters of Rosencrantz and Guildenstern."

"And why did you come here? I'm betting that you didn't come here for the waters."

The Professor smiled at my allusion to *Casablanca*. "Why yes," he countered, "but I was misinformed." He paused. "Alas—an honorary professorship entitles one to no tenure, no endowed chair, no pension. You see, my liver gave out before my yearning for knowledge did. And after a particularly pernicious attack, I realized I had to find a spot where the climate was salubrious and the expenses low." He took out his worn little leather change purse and emptied out its few coins. "And now I must confine myself to giving good advice." He sighed. "It consoles me for no longer being capable of setting a bad example."

"Excuse me, Professor, I wonder if you can remember anything more about Courtney and or perhaps speculate on where she might be."

"As to the young Americana, I would advise you to *cherchez l'homme*, and by that I mean, ask Ramon. I believe that Courtney was quite taken with him during her short stay. Not that she seemed to be overly particular or loyal in her affections. As to where Courtney is now, I have no idea."

"Professor, this is wonderfully helpful. I'll be taking Ramon's tour of Monte Alban this afternoon and I'll be sure to ask him. And now I must have some lunch before the bus leaves."

"After all Marjorie's warnings?" He raised his eyebrows, smiling. "Have you inspected the kitchens?"

"No," I said, "and I don't think I want to. Such things are best ignored in the general spirit of travel. Are you sure that you won't join me?"

The Professor eventually declined my offer and I left him and walked around the Plaza. I noticed that each cafe had its own special aura. The Cafe Portal, for example, boasted carved high-backed wooden chairs with leather seats, white tablecloths, and waiters, uniformed like Radio City Music Hall ushers. The Gelatao, on the other hand, had little white wobbly chairs, food-spotted yellow tablecloths and young boys dressed in Mickey Mouse tee shirts. There seemed less to live up to—so I slid onto one of the Gelatao's chairs.

I ordered a Corona. I have my food fetishes, too. I go for the specialties of the region—baked beans in Boston, salt water taffy in Atlantic City, and in Oaxaca, I would start with a Mexican beer. But I supposed I had better order some food as well. Idly, I looked at the menu.

Huevos Tirados
Cochinita Pibil
Menudo
Pollo Mole de Oaxaca
Frijolitos con hierba de conejo

I didn't know what any of these things were, but they all sounded good. I asked the waiter to pick something for me.

"Si, si Señorita—the menu turistico for today, our special—'pozole cooked with pig's head."' As a further enticement, he promised, "Everybody gets a piece of the ear."

"Thanks, that sounds wonderful," I said. Hmm. This was going to be a test of my principle of going native. I had just lifted my glass to lay down a nice coating of beer on my digestive tract, when suddenly a very old woman—her black rebozo shading her face—loomed beside me. A claw-like hand extended in front of my face and stayed there. By her silent accusatory presence, I was encouraged to drop a number of coins into her hand, and then, just as suddenly and silently as she had come, she moved away.

"Hello, Cousin," a voice beside me said. It was Archie Hayes, the Texas Ranger from the plane. "Did you enjoy the Hotel Casa Paradiso?"

"A little posh for my taste," I replied coolly. "Do you want to join me?" He sat down in another chair at my table.

A lovely but grime-covered little girl came by our table, selling "chicles," her mud-gray hands holding a tray on which were displayed a few sticks of gum. On my other side, I was now being besieged by two little boys, one holding a red piggy bank, the other an empty cardboard container of orange juice—both requesting "dinero." I gave each of them a handful of pesos. Another little girl came by selling individual cigarettes on a tray.

Archie looked around him angrily. "Mexico is having a population explosion. By 2005, there will be fifty million people in Mexico City alone. To you tourists—these ragged urchins are picturesque. To me—they need help." I looked at him, astounded. I certainly hadn't expected a lecture on morality from a Texan. Still, I couldn't agree more.

"And you know what kind of birth control they're taught?" He paused rhetorically. "Abstinence."

I looked suitably appalled. Large families were strolling by—one child by the hand, one held in the arms, and an infant hidden completely by a rebozo. "What do you do down here, Archie, anyway?" I asked curiously.

"I study the ruins of the past and present," he said cryptically.

It was an unanswerable remark, and there was an uncomfortable pause.

"I don't suppose that you've made any progress in your search for the missing gringa."

"Actually," I started to get up, "I'm following a lead right now. Need to catch a bus—"

Just then, as if he were a missile, a man ran at me, knocking me to the ground hard, and then kept running and vanished in the crowd as rapidly as he had appeared.

Archie quickly came to my side. "Are you hurt?" And when he saw that I was uninjured, "If I were you, I'd go easy on the Corona."

I got up slowly, brushing myself off. "Don't be stupid, Archie." I was really annoyed. "I didn't fall. Somebody knocked me down, and it seemed like he meant to do it on purpose."

He looked at me enigmatically. "I told you to be careful," he said.

18

Monte Alban

I WOULDN'T ADMIT IT to Archie, of course, but I didn't like being viciously knocked down one bit. True, it didn't seem likely that it was someone who had lured, kidnapped, or, God forbid, killed Courtney trying to scare me off the search. But, at the very least it was puzzling. No one on the street had seemed in such a hurry. As I walked to the corner of the Zocalo where I would catch the bus to Monte Alban, things in general began to look a little sinister to me, in spite of the sunlight and the crowds of people. The very old woman in the black rebozo with the gnarled hands—was she stalking me? Warning me? Even the enigmatic Ramon, whose tour I was about to take, seemed menacing. Was he luring me up to his turf for his own sinister purposes? What *did* he know about Courtney? Was she lost? Kidnapped? Or had she simply wandered off with some aging hippies who were, say, comparison-shopping for marijuana in Antigua at this very moment? Well, whatever the outcome, whatever the danger, I had resolved to keep up my search for her no matter what, until either I had found her or I had exhausted all leads. I had made a promise. It was my job and my responsibility. I would not wimp out. I decided to take some deep cleansing breaths and ignore my fears as much as I could.

The bus route up to Monte Alban was spectacular as we crawled up at what must have been at least a 45-degree grade—seemingly straight up, the road curving in hairpin turns around the side of the mountain. The first sight of the ruins at the top took my breath away.

There seem to be a few places on Earth where clearly gods may dwell, must dwell, might even be accessible to mortals. Delphi in Greece, with a view of Mt. Olympus, is surely one of them. Monte Alban is another. How to explain? The site is vast, on a huge leveled mountaintop, surrounded by purple mountains on all sides and then a vast blue-violet sky with wispy clouds. The ground is bare, covered with a green-brown scrub grass; the stones of the walls, monuments, and majestic pyramids are golden.

"The rectangular plaza," I read from my guidebook, "is 330 yards by 220 yards. Begun in 800 B.C. by the Zapotecs, the city rose to its peak in A.D. 500 and was abandoned mysteriously in A.D. 750. The whole site is on a perfect north/south orientation, except for one building, so called Mound J., which is on a 45-degree angle, thought to be an astronomical observatory." (This latter interpretation, in my view, is the last refuge of puzzled archeologists.)

"On the west side," the book continued, "is a temple with carved stone slabs—known as Temple of the Dancers—but now thought to be sacrificial figures. It is amazing how closely these figures resemble the current inhabitants of Oaxaca."

"The ball court is on the east. No one actually knows how the games were played, but many believe that the captain of the losing team was sacrificed. After 800, the place became essentially a burial place of the Mixtec Indians. More than 170 tombs have been excavated since the 19th century, and one, Tomb 7, is famous for its gold and jewels (now in the museum in Oaxaca) and tomb 104 is known for its figure of a priest in full ceremonial dress."

I was brusquely pulled from my reading by an insistent voice at my side:

"Buy a statue, lady? Old, old, very old." The speaker was Mexican, wearing a broadbrimmed straw hat against the sun, a faded blue shirt, and a kind of desperate expression. He was holding on a darkish cloth napkin a statue in clay, of a sort of warrior with a decorated breastplate and a large headdress.

Again and again, merchants kept offering me one artifact after another. Finally, when I was feeling put upon, a deep voice said, "Vayan, vayan."

I turned around and saw Ramon encouraging the vendors to try elsewhere.

"I'm glad to see you," I said. "I wasn't sure what to do about all of these merchants. What were they trying to sell me?"

"They try to sell to all the tourists. But whatever price anyone asks you, offer him about a third, and then settle between the two figures." Ramon laughed. "The men make clay figures and bury them in manure to age them, and then after a week or so, they do look old."

Perhaps I didn't want one after all.

"Never mind." He took my arm. "Let me show you the real glory of this place." He passed his hand proprietarily over the entire view. "Tell me, how do you like it?"

"Unbelievable," I said sincerely. This was about as far from middle-class McLean as I was likely ever to get.

He was pleased. "My ancestors, the Zapotecs, did all this, made all this. And now what are they?" He pointed derisively at the vendor.

It seemed a rhetorical question, so I stayed silent.

"Look around you. From 400 to 500 B.C. until the close of the tenth century, the Zapotecs settled here. They flattened the mountaintop, this entire space, some six hundred by a thousand feet—without any modern tools—and then they built a city here. They erected these colossal temples of rock—without cement—and decorated them with intricate patterns. Observe."

He turned me around to look eastward.

"They were wonderful mathematicians and astronomers. Look—that is their astronomical tower. All done by the Zapotecs." He continued: "Let me show you something even more interesting. Come with me." And he led me to the steps inside the temple. "This is the way to the tombs." And there, hidden under a trap door in the center of the temple court, were a few steep steps, the entrance to a burial vault.

"Who's buried here?" I asked.

"Probably high priests and tribal heads. In some of the graves, beautiful objects of art have been found. They show the Zapotecs' unrivaled artistic ability—gold jewelry, jade earrings, silver chalices, and hundreds of carved urns—like this one." He pointed to a stone vase in the corner. "Hundreds of urns, which held the ashes of the dead."

I looked at the urn more closely. It was in the shape of a nasty-looking creature—half animal, half-man.

"But now," with his arm around me, Ramon half-pushed, half-helped me down some more narrow steps—cleverly concealed by two columns and only partially visible. "This is named Grave number IV. Look around you. It's a miracle of preservation."

The walls were covered with red-brown, green, and blue figures in strange dress and even stranger positions. They postured, they knelt, they seemed to squat.

"Who are they?" I asked.

Ramon pointed to a painting of four men who, it appeared, were ready to walk out of the tomb. Near them on the other walls could be discerned the warm colors of more male and female figures. "They," said Ramon, "represent the nine Gods of Death with their wives."

I wanted to please him, to say that they were beautiful, but my overwhelming impression of the paintings was one of horror, of souls in pain, of demons and malignant gods and goddesses. I looked at Ramon and I saw a close resemblance between him and the figures on the wall—the same forehead, the same high-bridged aquiline nose. He himself could have sat for the portrait of the proud God of Death.

I began to feel my claustrophobia coming on. "I'm cold," I said. "Can we go up now?" It was good to leave the closeness of the subterranean vaults, clamber up the steps to once again breathe the clean, thin air of the mountaintop.

"Come," Ramon once again commanded. I followed his tall figure to a site behind one of the main buildings. "Look."

It appeared to be a basketball court with slanting walls.

"My ancestors played a game here in which no hands or heads were to be used, but only hips and shoulders. The game had a religious meaning and ended with the sacrificial death of some of the players. Imagine the spectators—priests—who from the temple terraces watched the game with intense interest."

"Who died? The winners or the losers?"

"We aren't sure," Ramon said. "But now observe this." And he pointed to an empty field with an urn in the middle. "This is another burial place. Here was a chocmal in which were placed the hearts of the sacrificed victims." The chocmal was a seated female figure reclining backwards and resting on her elbows. On her stomach was a flattened place that would have held the pulsating heart.

"It looks nasty to me," I said honestly, but the figure was beautiful.

"You don't understand." Ramon grabbed my arms and looked directly in my eyes. "The victim was proud to be chosen. He would allow the priest to seize him and to stretch him back over a stone. The priest would make an incision in his chest with a knife, and rip out the heart to be burned for the consumption of the gods."

In this long-abandoned field of the anonymous dead, Ramon's stern profile was silhouetted against the setting sun. He looked regal and implacable. In this place, I did not like to cross him. But I had some questions to ask.

"Ramon," I said, as forcefully as I could, "I came here to find out about Courtney."

"Encantadora," he held my arm gently at first and then his grasp tightened. "Do not ask too many questions. It is dangerous. Remember," he smiled enigmatically, "the gods do not like those who question their wisdom."

Ramon looked at his watch. "Six o'clock," he said. "We must go. Monte Alban closes now."

This time I held onto Ramon and stopped him. I was getting angry and impatient.

"You *do* know where Courtney is, *don't* you? I can feel it. And Marjorie knows, too."

He stood silent for a moment.

"I *will* find her, Ramon," I said. "Her mother needs to know." I sounded as firm and focused as I had ever been.

"I don't say that I know where she is," said Ramon slowly, "but I will try to find her. Meet me here tomorrow night. At ten o'clock."

"Please, Ramon. Tell me where she is now. Can I meet her tonight?"

"Tomorrow night, here, at ten o'clock," and he walked away quickly, with his beautiful head held high.

As I walked back to the bus stand, I looked carefully around me, as I was trained to do, for any signs of Courtney, and for people following me. I saw neither, although several women in black rebozos boarded the bus after me and followed me towards the Zocalo.

19

Skulls on My Pillow

AFTER MY BUS RIDE down the mountain, I stopped at the Plaza once again, this time to have supper. It was even brighter and noisier than before. Colored lights strung on wires over the streets spelled out *Feliz Navidad* while in the middle a neon Madonna and Child drifted back and forth.

On a gaily striped awning was emblazoned *Exquisitos Bunelos.* Under a canopy families were eating fried cakes and molasses. And after they had finished, each person took his bowl and smashed it in the street. I went over to an eight-year-old, happily throwing his earthenware dish in the street.

"Que pasa?" I asked in Spanish. "What are you doing?"

"We break our dish with a wish for a happy New Year," the little boy answered politely and then rushed back to the family fold.

Amid the gaiety and music—a marimba band was now playing "Valencia" on the bandstand and every now and again a firecracker went off—I returned to the Cafe Galateo and ordered some beef tacos and another Mexican beer, this time Dos Equis. Very satisfying. But as I walked back to my hotel, the gnawing feeling returned that Courtney was in danger and I wasn't moving as quickly as I had hoped.

My hotel, as I approached, looked dark and forbidding. No one was around. I went into the lobby and that was deserted, too. No one was there, not Mario, watching reruns of "Ponderosa Ranch," or even the bellboy with his headphones. I took my key from the board on which it was hanging with all the other keys—the Casa Paradiso was a trusting hotel—and walked across the courtyard to my room. The silence seemed unfriendly. I walked upstairs looking forward to the safety of my room.

My large old-fashioned key clanked as I tried to insert it into the lock. It didn't seem to fit. As last, I swung the door open, turned on the one overhead light, and immediately saw two strange objects on the worn green blanket. Cautiously, I edged up to them.

There on the bed were two life-size white skulls—one with the name of Courtney—and the other with my own name—Schaeffer—neatly printed in black at the base.

I gasped at first. Who had been in my room? What were those objects? What did they mean? Two white skulls. Somebody's idea of a practical joke? It wasn't funny. But then, practical jokes so seldom are. It looked more like a warning. A little hostile in intent, I thought, but a clue is a clue.

Without touching the skulls, I eyed them carefully. Then I inspected the room to see if anything of mine had been taken or anything of the intruder's had been left behind. In the end, I couldn't find anything either missing or extraneous. I guess anyone could have picked up my key at the unattended desk, deposited the skulls, and left quietly. Privacy and security were two luxuries in which the Hotel Casa Paradiso did not indulge.

Thoughtfully, I went downstairs again to the front office hoping that Mario had returned. There he was, calmly reading *La Prensa* behind the registration desk.

"Mario, I'm glad I found you."

"What passes, Señora? You find a cucaracha in your room?" He laughed, taking some justifiable enjoyment in the strange fears of the gringa.

"No cucaracha, but I did find two skulls in my room."

Mario's eyebrows went way up into his receding hairline. Now he was sure he had a woman on the verge of a nervous breakdown. He hastened to the water cooler and got a paper cup of water, but whether it was for me to drink or for him to throw over my head, I couldn't be sure.

I took the water gratefully, hoping that Mario wouldn't notice that I declined to drink it. I was sticking with beer for the moment.

Suddenly a light bulb illuminated itself in the fuzzy corners of my brain: Rosa Calderon. Rosa was jealous of Courtney. Was she trying to frighten Courtney and me away? And if so, did she know where Courtney was?

"Rosa," I said. "Where is she? I'd like to speak to her."

Mario was now really puzzled by my rapid and seemingly incoherent change of focus.

"Rosa?" he said. "Why do you ask about her?"

"Mario," I replied. "I just need to talk with her."

He looked away. "Ah, poor Rosa," he murmured. "She has suffered a susto."

"A susto? What's that?"

Mario sighed deeply. "A susto—a terrible fright. A 'shocking' you would call it. Pobre Rosita." He sighed again. "She is very ill. She is resting in her village."

"Her village? Is it far? I'd like to talk with her."

Mario seemed resigned to my whims. "She lives in the village of Teotitlan del Valle." He brightened. "That's the village of serapes. They make them there. You buy one and that makes the whole trip worthwhile."

"My purpose is to see Rosa," I said coldly.

"Yes, of course," he said, humoring my obsession. "About the skulls? Where do they sit?"

It was apparent from his patronizing tone that he thought the skulls were figments of my imagination. If they were no longer there, my credibility would be zero.

He followed me up the stairs to my room. I opened the door. Yes, they were still there.

A gust of laughter came from Mario. "You do not know what these are? It is jolly well a joke. See—the skull is made of sugar—" And to my surprise, he bit off a piece of the jaw labeled Schaeffer and began chewing it. "You see, we Mexicans do not fear the dead. We even have a holiday in November called 'The Days of the Dead.' On those days, we have a fiesta on the graves of our departed. We take food, drink, candles, flowers, and a guitar."

"To the cemetery?"

"Certainly to the cemetery. If this seems bad to you, it's because you think the dead want to be treated solemnly. But we think they want to eat, drink, and be merry like everyone else. Each house has an altar for the dead as well, and we offer them their favorite foods."

"You think the dead come back?"

"Of course. But if it is a 'good death,' they don't come back to haunt us. It is just a family visit."

"And the skulls—?"

"Skulls, certainly. And hard cookies that rattle, Dead Men's Bread, chocolate coffins, skeleton ballet dancers in papier-mache, and spun-sugar skulls. It's all part of our celebration."

I was interested, of course, but not impressed with this explanation. The Days of the Dead were over for the year. And one of those skulls had my name on it.

"Now, now, Señora, you are tired. You must try to sleep." He patted my arm. "Want a Pepsi?" This was clearly an American cure-all.

"No, thanks." I said. "I want to call my office." We went down again to Mario's station, I dialed the numbers, and I heard a great deal of static. I felt very far away from home.

This time Michael answered. "Schaeffer, how are you?" he asked with concern. I was really glad to hear his voice.

"I'm fine. But I haven't located Courtney. I do have leads, but nothing really tangible, and I'm wasting time, and—how is Will?"

"Well, good news on Will. He opened his eyes today for the first time. Marna was with him when it happened, and, actually, he said something rather strange."

"Are you going to make me beg?"

"He said, Marna thinks, 'her husband.' Not much, but the doctors think that it's a very good sign that he talked at all."

I felt incredibly relieved that Will had opened his eyes and spoken. I wanted now more than ever to find Courtney and make Will proud of me.

"That's wonderful, Michael. Did he say anything else? What do you think he meant?"

But neither Marna nor Michael had any idea. I pulled my thoughts back to Courtney.

"Did you talk to Courtney's mother and her father and stepfather?" I asked.

"Well, Marna tried Courtney's mother. She sounds depressed. But she couldn't reach father one or father two. The White House switchboard said simply that Montgomery Crawford was 'on travel,' and an answering machine picked up at Curtis Smith's house and he never returned the call."

"Hmm," I said, feeling paranoid, expecting the three parents to show up on my doorstep at any minute and demand Courtney. "Michael, remind me what are you supposed to do when things don't add up, when you don't know whom to trust, and you can't get a good lead?"

"Oh, it doesn't always work, but you know the prescribed drill. Write all the facts down, as if you were writing a report for a client. Make some hypotheses as to what happened. Then try them out."

"I know. That sounds so rational. But, Michael—there are sugar skulls on my bed, and a spirit in white called La Llorona seems to be haunting the hotel, and my major informant has gone home to her village on account of a 'susto,' a great fright. I hear Courtney's name a lot, but no one knows, or at least no one will tell me, where she is."

"Every puzzle has a solution," Michael said, I thought a little smugly.

"Easy for you to say. You get to do your detecting in your native tongue." I paused. " I miss you...and Marna," I added, trying to cover my emotional tracks.

"Me, too," Michael said noncommittally. It wasn't much, but I was greatly cheered just by talking with Michael. I felt his warmth over the miles through the wires. I didn't ask about his live-in lover Anna because I didn't want to discourage myself. Was I ready to fight for Michael? Would I have a chance?

"Schaeffer," Michael said after a short pause, "I meant to tell you that your ex-husband Nick called you at the office."

"What did he want?" I asked. I was surprised and curious. After all, the divorce was as good as over; the goods were divvied up. I couldn't imagine what more we had to say to one another.

"I don't know," Michael said. "I just told him that you were away on business."

"Did you tell him where?" All I needed was for Nick to turn up in Oaxaca and make a scene.

"Of course not," Michael said. "First rule of Private Eye etiquette."

"Well, that's a relief, anyway." I made a mental note to have Rachel, my friend and lawyer, check up on Nick when I got home.

There wasn't much more to say and I couldn't think up any more stalling tactics, so I said good-bye. Then I called goodnight to Mario, who had disappeared somewhere within, and went up to my room.

I had the usual battle with the faucet—a gurgle, then a snort, then a growl before the thin stream of brown water, and then I got into my white cotton nightgown. I picked up the skulls and examined them. Nothing tell-tale. Bought in any shop. I kept the Courtney one and ate the

Schaeffer. It certainly did seem like a warning of some sort. Keep out. Watch out. Don't meddle. Or what happened to Courtney will happen to you.

But what had happened to Courtney, and what exactly was I meddling in? It was hard to stop doing something you didn't know you were doing. Remembering Michael's advice, I took out my note pad, and wrote down everything I could think of: Persons involved:

1. Courtney Smith (missing)
2. Courtney's Mother, Emily Crawford
3. Curtis Smith, C's Father
4. Montgomery Crawford, C's Stepfather
5. Mario Bueno—any possible motive not known
6. Marjorie Daws—jealousy? Possessiveness?
7. Ramon Gonzalez—romance gone bad?
8. Rosa Calderon—jealousy?
9. The Professor—money?

Hypotheses as to Where Courtney is Now:

1. Courtney is traveling in, say, Guatemala?
2. Courtney was a victim of crime? A random crime? Political crime?
3. Courtney has been kidnapped (why? by whom?)
4. Courtney is in voluntary hiding with someone she came to meet (why? with whom, if anyone?)

Reasons for Courtney's Traveling to Oaxaca:

1. To enjoy the sun?
2. To get, use, and smuggle drugs?
3. To infuriate parents?
4. To have a romantic fling with Latino men like Ramon?
5. To meet someone?

I had every reason to think that Courtney was involved with one or several men. But who, how, and why? Casual romance? And why would she have come to Oaxaca in the first place? I was thoroughly unenlightened by this paper exercise.

I turned out the light and got into my narrow bed. Familiarity with the Hotel Casa Paradiso had not increased my affection for it. Tomorrow morning, though, I thought to myself, I would visit Rosa in her village, and then at 10:00 tomorrow night, I would meet Ramon at Monte Alban. One of the two would surely lead me to Courtney.

Damn. I had been in Oaxaca nearly two days and had so little to show for it. I drifted into a troubled sleep, trying my best to win an ancient game of soccer in which the rules were unknown to me and there was no ball.

20

The Fright

AT 11:30 THE NEXT MORNING I went to the Oaxaca Central Bus Station to get the second-class bus—there was no other kind—to Teotitlan del Valle, Rosa Calderon's village.

I joined a group of waiting Mexicans, many seeming to be on their way back from the morning market. The group was smiling and seemed friendly—until the signal to go aboard. Then whoever or whatever was in their path to the open bus door was as dead meat. A housewife with bundles elbowed a teenage boy in the groin. A young man trampled on what appeared to be his elderly, gray-haired grandmother. I was pushed along in the forward surge of humanity, and, after a bad three minutes, finally found myself more or less sitting down.

There were at least three people to each green painted two-seater bench. I had been pushed into a corner of the front seat and now was sitting beside a pregnant woman with a six-month-old baby in her lap and a three-year-old boy half in mine.

When the bus was packed, babies on laps, men, women, and children standing in the aisles, the conductor decided that this constituted "full" and slammed the doors shut. However, this was only phase one. Now vendors were passing by the sides of the bus selling ice cream and cold drinks through the open windows. I felt something cold on my back and turned around. It was only a little ice cream. But two benches behind me I thought that I saw the elderly lady beggar in the black serape from the Zocalo. Was she following me? Or just heading home? Every once in a while I felt a slight peck in the back of my neck. Finally I turned around to stare directly into the beady eyes of an irate chicken. Her owner laughed and apologized, "Lo siento," and pushed the offending bird back into the basket from which his head had emerged.

I turned quickly and looked in front. The bus driver's station was decorated like a shrine. On the left above the steering wheel was a decal of a Madonna and Child. The glass knob of the gearshift was covered with a picture of a saint. Finally, in the center of the windshield was a photo of Bruce Lee. Hey, whatever would help to get us there safely. Finally, the driver climbed in and started our ancient bus with a strong lurch forward. Its roof was sagging under bales of alfalfa, and its insides were crammed with the aforementioned people plus small pigs, turkeys, and cases of soft drinks. Through the cracks in the floor, dust came up in clouds. There was some strangled coughing and some irritated turkey pecks at my bare legs. But the general atmosphere, unlike the cold silence of a packed Washington Metro, was festive.

The bus driver was a virtuoso. He played his vehicle like a violin. He swerved, he turned, he changed gears. Every once in a while on the narrow winding road, a man on a burro or an ox cart seemed to come directly in front of our bus, but at the last moment our driver always eluded them. No matter that the bus was old, the road rutted, and the obstacles many, this driver was a master.

At last we came into the outskirts of Teotitlan. The town appeared deserted. Only now and then I caught glimpses of people hidden behind a hedge of cactus, some of them busy at a loom or spinning or just sitting and watching the bus go by. But as we came into the heart of the town, I saw that each house was a display store for the hand-woven and individually designed serapes, decorated with everything from traditional motifs in black, white, and brown to elaborate copies of Picasso.

Following Mario's directions, I waited until the bus stopped at the center of the town. Three old men sat on a bench outside a building labeled "Jail," and I asked the one closest the way to Rosa Calderon's house. He pointed to a small side street off the main road; I walked down it until I reached a small wooden house with weathered boards and a tin roof. In the front yard was a lone chicken; on the side of the house a dismembered green Buick lay on its side. A donkey was tethered by the front door.

I knocked briskly and was greeted by a robust young woman, who looked at me questioningly.

"I'm an amiga de Rosa," I told her. "My name's Schaeffer Brown."

"I am Soledad, Rosa's sister. Come in."

The room was dimly lit, the shutters closed, I guessed, against the hot sun. I walked forward on the dirt floor, strewn with bags of corn, until I saw Rosa. Instead of the vigorous and passionate young woman who had told me about La Llorona just a day before, I saw a wretched figure on the floor, her neck and head bent over almost as if she had stiffened in that position.

"Rosa, it's Schaeffer Brown, from the Hotel Casa Paradiso. Are you all right," I asked softly, kneeling beside her.

Mercifully, Rosa half-straightened up and put her hand out to me. "Oh, Señora, you have come to see me." I did not feel proud of the real reason for my visit, but I needed Rosa's help.

"I suffer from the susta," Rosa went on. "I was poisoned by witchcraft." Could this be the same Rosa Calderon who had learned near-perfect English at Catholic school and wanted to be a teacher?

Suddenly remembering her duties as a host, Rosa asked her sister to bring me something to drink.

I let Soledad know that this was not necessary, but she was adamant. "We will drink to your salud," she said. Soledad returned with a small glass filled with yellowish-green liquid.

I hesitated, but I knew that it was my duty to accept it, just as it was their duty to offer it. Had the drink always been yellowish-green or had it turned? I said, "Salud," closed my eyes, and took a drink. It was straight alcohol. And not bad either.

Soledad patted me on the back. "Gracias. You do honor to our house."

"But what has made you sick, Rosa?" I said, taking another taste.

Rosa shook her head. "A bruja—a witch—has sent an aigre—bad air—into my body."

Speaking of air, the room was feeling awfully stuffy. I noticed that every now and then a curl of pungent smoke permeated the space.

Rosa seemed to read my mind. "It's copal, incense. If I burn copal, perhaps the smoke will remove the sickness from my body."

"But how was this done to you?"

"The evil eye."

"But how exactly?"

"Someone tricked me."

"Who?"

She shrugged her shoulders. "Perhaps your American friend Courtney or another woman—so she can have El Coyote to herself. Perhaps La Llorona. Quien sabe?"

I tried to use this mention of Courtney to further my inquiries. "Have you seen Courtney, Rosa? Did you see her put a spell on you?"

"I am not sure. I saw someone in white."

"When did you see her?"

"Oh, often, every time." She sat down again.

I sighed to myself. This line of questioning wasn't going anywhere. "Can I do something to help you? Can I take you to a doctor?"

"Doctor?" Rosa laughed scornfully. "What I need is a curandera. Will you help me go?"

"Yes, of course." I thought that I was beginning to understand the nature of Rosa's illness and to empathize with her. Perhaps "susta" was just another word for acute depression, or breakdown, or Loss of Nerve, as I called it. I was very familiar with the feeling.

Although the sun was shining, Rosa got a shawl, and we walked slowly, half-limping, further down the same side street to the curandera's house.

At the house of the curandera, Rosa stopped at the door and explained, "The curandera will suck out the things that the witch has thrown into the air and made enter me." Then she knocked and a very old woman opened the door. She looked older than anyone I can remember, older than the pyramids of Monte Alban. Her fine skin was criss-crossed by a thousand lines, her face an ancient parchment of wrinkles. What I noticed at last with a start, when the curandera lifted her face to us, was that the curandera's eyes, amid the myriad wrinkles, were smoothly covered by a blue-white film. There were no pupils at all. The curandera must have been completely blind.

I hesitated briefly as the curandera silently held the door open for Rosa and me. Why was I frightened by this very old woman? Was it her age itself that scared me? Or what she had seen in her life? Or her supposed magical powers, which, in this setting, it was hard to be too smug about? Would she be using her powers for good or ill? Or was it simply the sightless gaze that scared me, a gaze that could see nothing except what was inside or unseeable?

I had no time to hesitate for long, but followed Rosa into the small house. It looked a lot like Rosa's, in fact, except that the walls were hung with dried or drying bunches of herbs and flowers. Also a large rough-hewn wooden chest held boxes of all sizes and bottles filled with colored liquids of unknown origins and effects. None of the bottles had labels.

Apparently, the curandera had divined what Rosa's sickness was because she asked for no particulars. Silently, she motioned us to sit down on the floor next to a small fireplace.

We three sat cross-legged, the bright fire bringing the indoor temperature of the house to about 110 degrees Fahrenheit. I began to sweat and felt the beginnings of my old claustrophobia welling up. This made me even more apprehensive. What was that green drink Soledad had given me? I vowed to leave the curandera's house without imbibing anything further.

The heat seemed to increase as the curandera reached into the folds of her long brown dress, extracted a small packet, and hurled it into the fire. I startled as it exploded, crackled, and hissed, releasing a strong unfamiliar medicinal smell into the room.

The curandera then spoke rapidly to Rosa in an Indian language that I could not understand at all. Rosa bent her head and closed her eyes. The curandera then murmured a long incantation in which I could pick out Rosa's name. I tried to change my position and re-cross my legs but found that unaccountably I could not move. I was frozen in my own prison of sweat.

Then, from another pocket of her voluminous brown dress, the curandera withdrew an egg. With a few more words, she instructed Rosa to lie back, her head on a rough hemp pillow. Then the curandera rubbed the egg slowly over Rosa's face and neck, then her arms and breasts, then her torso and thighs. It seemed creepy to me, sensual certainly, and almost sexual in a way. I wanted to look away but couldn't. All the while the curandera's mouth was moving silently, a slight smile on her lips, her cauled blue-white eyes looking upward without seeing. Rosa turned her head from side to side and moaned. I prayed silently that the ritual would end before anything even creepier happened.

At last the ceremony was over. The curandera whispered for Rosa to sit up and to open her eyes. Then, with a quick practiced movement, she cracked the egg open on a tin dish next to the fire. A large yolk rolled out intact amid the viscous white. From the broken egg, the curandera seemed to extract a small rusty nail, which she held up to Rosa, unsmilingly, for her inspection.

Rosa nodded comprehendingly at the sight of the egg and the rusty nail. She straightened up—her voice had become stronger. "I feel better," she said. In Spanish she said, "I thank you, Señora Curandera," and took a roll of well-worn bills and gave them to the old woman. Then she bent down and kissed the curandera's gnarled hand. Still unsmiling, the curandera got up with difficulty, led us back to the front door, and opened it. The daylight and the cool air came as a relief to me and I was beginning to shake off the cobwebs of ancient ritual and magic.

I was unprepared, therefore, when the curandera turned her filmy, sightless eyes toward me and pointed one finger at me, firmly touching my chest.

"Beware, Señora," she said in the same quiet raspy voice. "*You* are in danger." Leaving me open-mouthed in shock, she turned slowly and carefully closed the door behind her.

I hate to admit it, but I was unnerved. I had erroneously allowed myself to believe that the curandera was not aware or at most hardly aware of my presence during the ceremony. I swallowed hard. I knew in my mind that I could get a more accurate fortune from a weighing machine, but I couldn't help believing her. Her cautionary words were so gratuitous and unexpected. It seemed not at all unlikely that she could sense something about me. I left with Rosa and walked down to the main street in a much sobered frame of mind.

Rosa, on the other hand, seemed to feel much better. For her, the encounter must have been a salubrious combination of psychotherapy, aromatherapy, hypnosis, and massage. She walked me back to the bus stop where I would catch my ride back to Oaxaca, and we waited on a bench near the jail, shaded by an old tree.

"Rosa," I said slowly, "I'm very glad that you're feeling better." I paused. "Would you know what the curandera meant about my being in danger?"

Rosa shrugged and shook her head.

Still feeling shaky, I put all my energies into refocusing on the task at hand. I needed to use these last few minutes to learn anything I could about Courtney. "Rosa," I began, leading up to the subject slowly, "do you live with your sister, Soledad?"

"I was married," answered Rosa, "and I lived with my husband and my husband's family. But my husband was a bad man. He beat me."

"I'm sorry." It seemed weak, but I could think of nothing else to say. At any rate, I was glad to see the characteristic anger and energy returning slowly to Rosa's voice.

"Then I meet El Coyote, and he showed me to be proud—proud because I am true Zapotec." Suddenly she slumped, and I was afraid she was going to revert to her pre-curandera state. "But now he never comes to me anymore. Always he came to me at night—but now no more. Other women—your Courtney, too—took him away. If I find them—" her vigor had definitely returned and she made a sign of slashing a throat—"I will kill them with my machete."

"Do you know where Courtney is now? When did you last see her?"

Rosa narrowed her lips. "When I find her, I will kill her. I will kill for my Coyote. I do not find fault with him. He is the way he is because his tono is the coyote."

"Tono?"

Rosa laughed scornfully at my ignorance. "Everybody has a tono."

"What is it?"

"A tono is an animal soul put in a baby when it is in the mother's stomach."

"How do you know what your tono is?"

"Many ways. You feel it or dream it. Sometimes when a baby is born, the padre keeps naming over animals and birds, and the one he says at the time the baby comes—that is the tono of the baby. Or sometimes—the new baby is left alone in a room the first night after it is born. Around the mat on which it sleeps, the padre sprinkles ashes, and when the sun come up, he looks at the ashes to find an animal's mark which has been near the baby in the night."

So a tono was an animal double. The idea intrigued me. I wondered what mine was. "Do people ever see their tono?"

"Oh yes, many times. And always just before you die," Rosa crossed herself, "your tono comes and gives you warning."

"What is your tono, Rosa?"

"My tono is a black cat," she said proudly. "All people who can see the dead have black cat tono."

This whole visit—Rosa's illness, her miraculous cure, her tono—was confusing me more than clearing things up.

"Rosa," I began, trying another tack. "I think I've seen La Llorona."

"When?" She didn't sound at all surprised.

"Two nights ago. In the courtyard. And then, Rosa, when I came to my room last night, there were two skulls sitting on my blanket." My story sounded preposterous even to me.

"Dios mios," Rosa looked serious. "You must take care. The evil spirits—they work against you. The curandera said so."

By this time my bus had arrived, and with most of my questions unanswered, I prepared to board. Fortunately, at this hour not many people were going to accompany me to the city, so I was assured of a leisurely and comfortable ride. Rosa and I parted in a somber mood.

"I will help you," Rosa called to me through the open window. "I will come to work tomorrow and together we will watch for La Llorona."

I had entered Rosa Calderon's world of magic, tonos, and curanderas. But I had precious little to show for it beyond a very uneasy feeling.

21

Monte Alban, by Night

I GOT BACK to my room a little hot, dusty, and discouraged at my wasted morning. I had had more than a large enough dose of black magic. I realized that life here was hard and that people felt at the mercy of forces they could not control, but didn't I feel the same way? Only the thought of tonight's meeting with Ramon kept me motivated. In some corner of my mind, I expected Ramon to lead me to Courtney and unravel this distressing puzzle. At the very least I expected some information about her. Why all this secrecy? What was going on?

As I prepared to leave my room, a large black cat appeared on the threshold, blocking my way. It hissed, then turned its head and looked at me with what seemed like a spiteful expression.

The black cat, I remembered, was Rosa's tono, and darned if the cat didn't resemble Rosa, too—with the same dark eyes and sleek hair. Even the way it sat imperiously in the doorjamb, licking an injured paw. I just hoped Rosa wouldn't tell me the next day that her foot hurt.

I had to pass the cat to get out of the door. "Excuse me," I said, catching myself too late. I was having a conversation with a cat. I really had to get out of this place.

At 10 p.m. sharp, I stood waiting for Ramon at the bus stop at Monte Alban.

"Querida," came a voice from the darkness. Ramon clearly enjoyed appearing mysteriously. "You're here, Querida." The very fact that I had come seemed to him to establish our relationship on a different, more intimate basis. And wasn't 'Querida' some inappropriate term of endearment? I had to nip this attitude in the bud.

"Courtney," I reminded him. "I came to find out about Courtney."

He put his finger to his lips. "We must be very quiet." I guessed it was no time to argue. Silently he led me up a hill. We were at the back of the ruins, which had been fenced in by barbed wire. Unerringly Ramon went to a spot where the wire had been severed and then carefully placed together to prevent discovery. With his gloved hand, he lifted the wire and we crawled under it.

In the moonlight he led me to an opening in the ground. Pulling aside some bushes, he revealed steps leading downward into blackness. I was not really keen on going underground, what with my incipient claustrophobia and all, and I was particularly not elated to be going there with someone who seemed to think that we were out on a date. But, hey, what would V.I. Warshawski have done?

Down and around we went, through a labyrinth of steep stairs and narrow passages until at last we came to a mid-sized room. It had air from an opening in the ceiling and as for light—Ramon took a beautiful tin candleholder from a corner and lit its many candles. "This," said Ramon, "is Tomb V."

Ramon touched my hair. "As soon as I saw you, I knew you were a gentle soul, able to understand me and my people." He got out a pipe, which he stuffed with something that looked like tobacco, but might have been something stronger. Once lit, its scent, now familiar to me only from free concerts on the Mall, was clearly marijuana. Ramon inhaled deeply and handed the pipe to me. "Smoke," he said. "It will give you sweet dreams."

I took the pipe and drew on it. I swear that I didn't inhale—following the tradition of great people before me—but the smoke was really powerful, and I felt just a little strange.

"You must help me," he said, "to bring back the glory of the Zapotecs.

How we have fallen! Our very bodies have diminished in size. Our women are no longer so beautiful. Our men no longer so strong." He became agitated. "In an ancient Zapotec tomb, I found a huge grinding stone. Today it would take two of our men to use it."

It was clear now that I was in the presence of a lunatic. A lunatic with a mission. While he talked, he kept handing me the pipe and then taking it back. To punctuate each statement, he would inhale deeply. Fortunately, my role seemed to be merely that of an auditor, struggling to stay awake.

I was starting to feel a sort of pleasant numbness when Ramon stood up and said grandly, "My name is El Coyote, leader of my people. Coyote is my tono. It was so ordained."

This pronouncement jolted me out of my agreeably relaxed state. Ramon Gonzalez was El Coyote? The El Coyote who was Rosa's lover? And Marjorie's co-worker in the library? And my knowledgeable guide to Monte Alban? I couldn't believe that I hadn't put this together. I felt too stupid to live. Too shortsighted to be allowed to drive a car. Too obtuse to be let outside without a chaperone. I would have gone on excoriating myself, but this was not to be.

Ramon leaned over and shook me hard. "Now," he said, "I will dance for you. For you alone, mi corazon, I will do the plume dance."

I remembered the plume dance from my travel book. Stupidly I asked, "But doesn't it tell the story of the Spanish soldiers overcoming the Zapotec warriors?"

"It's a lie!" He clenched his fists. "The white men have corrupted our native dance and made it seem like a triumph of white Christianity. But Cortes only defeated us because he was helped by this traitorous concubine Malinche." He pushed me down on a stone step. "Sit now and watch."

He took off his long poncho and suddenly he revealed himself as a figure of splendor.

Everything about him glittered. He wore a red silk shirt and pants of red brocade with goldfringed tiers. His intricately patterned metal breastplate, made up of gold and silver circles set in zigzagged patterns, reflected the flickering lights of the candles.

Then with great care he put on his huge headdress—at least three feet in diameter—made of feathers, scarlet, orange, green, yellow, and purple. Amid this rainbow twinkled mirrors, which repeated and sharpened the colors. All this plumage arose from a golden headband.

Around his smooth dark muscled arms were tied bright silk kerchiefs. On his feet he wore embroidered sandals. In his right hand he carried a huge shield and in his left a sharp curved ceremonial knife. I sat there, dazzled. It was like having a picture on an ancient vase come to life.

Ramon slowly and solemnly turned around in front of me. "I do my dance in a different way—a way that reveals the truth. Cortes arrives—we have a battle for the land—but instead of the submission of the Indians to the Cross, in my dance, the black Cristo Esquipulas gives the land back to the Indians to whom it will belong eternally."

Slowly Ramon started to dance. He would make a small movement forward, whirl completely around, crouch on one knee, and turn, then make another forward movement. He moved gracefully through the cavernous room with intricate steps. Soon he started turning faster and faster until he reached a frenzy of passion. He seemed to have been transformed into a figure of fury. He grabbed my arms and stared into my face. There was no recognition in his eyes. Finally he bent my head back, held me around the throat and readied his knife. "Traitorous Malinche, what have you done to me, to the Zapotecs?" He held the knife to my throat.

"Ramon," I said, willing him to listen. "I'm not Malinche. Let go of me!"

He paid no attention.

"I—El Coyote—living head of my tribe—take you. You are mine." Suddenly, Ramon kissed me hard and clasping my neck tightly, he lifted the knife to strike at my heart.

The kiss and the raised knife brought me to my senses. Using my best technique from the three required hours of self-defense class, I made a fist with my right hand and jabbed at Ramon's Adam's apple with my knuckles. At the same time, I lifted my right knee to his groin. The shock and pain of these maneuvers made him reel backwards, but I realized that he would recover rapidly and that I would have to get away fast. I ran towards the steps and climbed quickly, striving to see the stars or moonlight. Just as I reached the second flight of steps, I saw something small and yellow on the floor. I scooped it up as I ran and kept running till I had reached the top of the stairs, crossed the plaza, and struggled through the barbed wire surrounding the site. I looked around me to see if anyone was following and then I started running again and kept on all the way down the mountain. I did not look back. When I got down to the bus stop, I flopped down on a bench and caught my breath. I thought that I was going to throw up, what with fear, and the smoke, and the exertion, but I put my head back and took some deep cleansing breaths. There were a few people at the stop and a streetlight.

Then I remembered the small yellow object I had picked up in the tomb and thrust into my pocket. I took it out and inspected it. It was a matchbook from J. Gilbert's restaurant in McLean, Virginia.

22

Darkness Before Dawn

◗ ON THE BUS back to the Zocalo, I had time to think. I hadn't actually seen Courtney, but I had to believe that she had been there with Ramon recently—perhaps staying with him. The matchbook from a McLean restaurant was simply too great a coincidence to mean anything else. But why was she there with Ramon a.k.a. El Coyote, a pretty strung-out if impassioned advocate for the Zapotec people? And, most importantly, where was Courtney now?

I got off the bus and picked up a taxi back to the Hotel Casa Paradiso. In the taxi, I thought about what else I had learned. That Ramon was connected to Courtney and to Rosa as El Coyote, her faithless lover, and to Marjorie as well. For Ramon, her protegé at the library seemed to have a very special place in her heart, perhaps something more even than a colleague and pupil. Had Courtney been frightened off or hurt either by Rosa or Marjorie? Or, God forbid, had Ramon/El Coyote hurt Courtney in one of his Zapotec fantasies, such as the one I had participated in unwillingly tonight? What would have happened to me in the next act if I hadn't had those three required hours of self-defense?

But none of this, none of it—though coherent in itself—explained why Courtney had come to Oaxaca in the first place. I felt no closer to learning that or to finding Courtney than I had been when I arrived.

It was after 1 a.m. when I trudged up the steps to the Casa Paradiso. I was weary and discouraged and ready to call for reinforcements. What were the Oaxacan police doing anyway? And what about that reputable

Oaxacan detective agency that Michael had been supposed to find and contact for me? If I could remember which way the time zones worked, I was definitely calling the office to complain.

As I walked up to Mario's desk, now deserted, to use the telephone, I was startled to see Rosa, rising like a ghost from a chair in the lobby.

"Where were you?" Rosa asked accusingly. She now stood in front of me, her eyes narrowed with suspicion. "Where were you?" I sighed. In my current frame of mind, a confrontation with Rosa was not what I needed.

"Well," I began slowly. This was going to be hard to explain. I decided on a different tack. "Anyway, what are you doing here? I thought that you were coming tomorrow."

"I came early," she replied. Then she looked me straight on. "I followed you to Monte Alban," she said. "I saw you meet my Coyote. You are not my friend. You are just like Courtney and Marjorie and the other women. You all want my Coyote for yourself."

"No, Rosa. I was only looking for Courtney. Ramon said that he would help me find her."

Rosa paused, reflected, then shook her head. "You are not my friend. I followed you to Monte Alban. I saw you meet mi amor."

"Rosa, I understand that this is hard to believe, but I only met Ramon tonight because he said that he would tell me about Courtney. When I left him (I didn't think it relevant to mention his condition), Ramon had told me nothing, but I did find this matchbook." I showed it to her. "It's from the town that Courtney comes from. So I have to think that Courtney was there with Ramon and maybe still is and may even be in danger."

The last possibility didn't seem to cause Rosa much anxiety.

"As soon as it's morning, Rosa, I'm going to go back to look for Courtney. Do you want to come with me?"

No answer.

"And maybe we should hold Ramon just a little bit responsible for all this—with Courtney and the other women? In my country, a woman would kick a man's sorry bottom out the door for being so unfaithful."

Still, no answer.

"Okay. Don't answer me now. I need to call my office anyway."

I dialed the office number and got a recorded message. Drat. Who knows what time it was in McLean?

"Rosa," I said, "I'm going up for a short nap. I'll be ready to go back to Monte Alban as soon as it's light, and I'd like to have you come with me if you'd like."

Rosa said nothing, and I walked wearily up to bed.

23

Daylight

I WAS AWAKENED at 1:00 in the afternoon by the sun streaming in my window. I felt terrible. My neck was stuck at a hideous angle, and my stomach was queasy in the extreme. I felt still worse when I remembered what had happened last night, where I was, and that I had to return to Monte Alban to find Courtney.

Slowly, slowly, I moved my head, creating a sharper pain in my neck and causing what seemed like all the little grains of sand in my head to shift painfully to the other side. I had to guess that I had taken in more of Ramon's smoke than I had thought. I was just raising myself up in stages to an elbow-leaning position when a vision of Courtney's face danced before my eyes. I willed my eyes open and sat up in bed, alert.

After what I had gone through last night, I knew that Courtney really was in trouble—whether from Ramon and his knife-wielding alter-ego, or from Rosa and her machete, or from some as-yet-unidentified source who had led Courtney here in the first place. And with someone most likely dogging my steps as well, one or both of us were just begging to land in some deep yogurt. It wasn't just the curandera's warning to me or even the craziness with Ramon last night. It was now that Courtney had been missing for a significant amount of time, and that each hour that passed made it statistically less likely that I would find her alive.

I knew that Courtney had been up to Ramon/El Coyote's lair. The yellow matchbox from J. Gilbert's restaurant wouldn't lie about that. I had to go back there and pick up the trail.

As fast as I could move my logy body, I got up, pulled on jeans, sandals, and a light-tan tee shirt. I splashed what ought to have been cold water, but was in fact the usual tepid, brownish liquid, on my face. That helped. I bounded—well, walked quickly—down the stairs of the Hotel Casa Paradiso and saw no sign of either Rosa or Mario. I made my way as quickly as I could to the Zocalo, and a quick black coffee and sweet roll later, I had hailed a taxi and was on my way back up the mountain to Monte Alban.

This time I knew the territory better. I avoided the merchants of dung-aged pottery either by scowling at them or by avoiding their gaze. I looked quickly around and saw no sign of Ramon with a tour group. Then I retraced Ramon's and my steps of last night, under the break in the barbed wire, and through the back entrance of the ruins. I followed what I thought was our trail last night to Tomb V.

The dry grass had been worn pathlike by several comings and goings. About 30 yards down the path, out of sight of the tourist hordes and behind one of the large pyramids, the trail broadened into a kind of odd-sided oval space. If I had to guess, it looked like a struggle had taken place there and that someone had fallen, creating an irregular patch of dried, matted grass. I kneeled to look more closely, and to my dismay, I saw a brownish stain in the ground, possibly blood.

As I continued to examine the area, it became clear that the matted grass continued off down a little ridge. It was either a separately worn path, or, seeing that the grass was bending in one direction, something or someone had been dragged down the hill. I forced myself to follow this trail down, wanting and not wanting to see where it led. The hill became steeper and, near the bottom of a ditch-like hollow, I saw something that I hope to God never to see again.

It was the still figure of a young woman face down in the dirt. Her hands were tied behind her back; her feet were tied togther, too, with strong rope. Her neck was at an awkward angle, and her face was half-turned up and half-buried in the sandy dirt and dry grass. I could see as I walked closer that her mouth had been taped shut and that there was dried blood on the back of her head, clotted in her streaked brown hair, just above her right ear.

I knew in my heart that this was Courtney, and I prayed and hoped against hope that she wasn't dead. It took all of my courage to scramble down the last steps to her and kneel next to her. But immediately I could hear her troubled breathing and thanked the powers that be that she was still alive! I had come in time, before she died of thirst or loss of blood or even an attack of wild animals that still roamed these hills. A coyote would have been most appropriate.

Working quickly, I got out my Swiss army knife and cut the ropes that bound her hands and feet. Then I turned her over as gently as I could, cradling her head on my right arm. There in front of me was the face that had always been in my thoughts, the face that I had been chasing down relentlessly as if in a bad dream. Courtney's face. She looked like her picture: thin, young, regular features, brown hair with gold streaks, but now beaten and vulnerable.

I shook her gently and said her name. She seemed to respond to her name and struggled to open her eyes. When she did, she looked at me, terrified.

"It's okay," I said. "You're safe now. Your mother sent me here to find you." I paused. "I'm going to take the tape off your mouth now. Hope it doesn't sting." I grasped an edge, gave it a hard tug, and ripped it off with a painful tearing sound.

"My head," Courtney said first as she tried to speak. She must have been parched. I kicked myself for not thinking to bring water.

"Courtney," I said, trying to sound calm, "how do you feel? Are you okay? I'm just going to take a quick peek at your head and see what seems to be the matter." I checked lightly and carefully through the matted hair and, to my relief, found only a large bruise and shallow abrasion, not a bullet hole or anything. It looked like Courtney had been hit by a hard object, a rock, or the butt of a gun.

"You were hit on the head, Courtney. It doesn't look too bad. You'll be fine." Hit on the head, I thought, dragged down into a ditch, and left to die. "Do you know who did this to you?"

She shook her head carefully, mutely, afraid to look.

"Here," I said, sounding inevitably like a hospital nurse. "Let's try to sit up. We've got to get you out of this dry gully and into a wet Corona," I misquoted for my own amusement. To lighten the mood, you know. "My name's Schaeffer Brown, by the way. Do you know who I am?"

"Sort of," said Courtney sullenly, but I could hardly blame her for her lack of enthusiasm. Her head must have felt like the wrong end of a fraternity hazing. "I knew that you were looking for me and figured that my mom sent you." Unexpectedly, she started to sob.

"Hey, hey," I said soothingly. "You're safe now. Let's try to get you on your feet." I was relieved that her cognitive functioning seemed unimpaired and that she seemed capable of movement. With my help, she stood up stiffly and tried to stretch her arms. We struggled up the hill together, I half-pushing her up, and then we followed the matted grass back to the barbed wire and then to the bus stop. I bought Courtney two bottles of Coca-Cola from a vendor and told her to sip them slowly. Then I hailed a taxi and we sped down the mountain to the Zocalo.

I asked the driver to let us off at one of the fanciest hotels in Oaxaca, the Hotel Camino Real on the Calle Cinque de Mayo. I had remembered it from my guidebook and had passed it several times. It dated from the sixteenth century and had formerly been the convent Santa Catalina. This girl needed some privacy, some protection, some real American food, and a good hot shower, none of which could be had at the Hotel Casa Paradiso for love or money. Besides, staying in a big, old convent sounded safe.

I booked a room with double beds and marched Courtney through the plant-filled lobby, up one flight of stairs, and into a grand room with a gorgeous marble and black tile bathroom. It had a working shower and many plump white towels. I helped Courtney out of her very dirty clothes and ran a tepid shower for her. There was vanilla-scented exfoliating soap and mango-scented shampoo.

Next I called room service and asked them to send up a six-pack of bottled water, two hamburgers, two pieces of chocolate cake, and something from the gift shop for a young woman to wear—a cover-up or sundress or the like. I told them to put it all on my bill. I wasn't going to let Courtney out of my sight even for a second.

When the room service clerk brought up our food and drink, I sent him down with a large tip and with Courtney's old clothes to be laundered. It really was nice to be on Courtney's mother's expense account. What with the exchange rate and all, she would hardly see this as overspending. I knew that she would have done the same to get Courtney back home safely, in good health, and in clean clothes.

I knocked on the bathroom door and handed in Courtney's new outfit. It was a simple white shift with turquoise piping and looked quite nice. Then I waited for Courtney to emerge. The room itself was handsome if you liked convent-style architecture as holiday accommodations. The walls were yellow ocher-colored stone and were curved in odd places. The accents in the room—of the couch, bedspreads, and pictures—were colorful. It was true that the room was large and the stone walls cool, but the room still had a disconcertingly crypt-like quality, not tailor-made for someone with my claustrophobic tendencies.

About ten minutes later, Courtney came out of the bathroom looking amazingly good. Her long hair was shiny and combed straight down her back and the white dress set off her lightly tanned skin. Ah, the resilience of youth.

"How's your head, Courtney? Can I take another look?"

"It's a little sore, but I think it's okay," she said quietly. My check confirmed a nasty bruise but no more.

"Are you hungry?" I asked. Courtney went straight to the table and scarfed her hamburger and piece of chocolate cake between swigs of bottled water. She drank a second bottle straight down, raising the water table in her system considerably. I ate my hamburger and cake, too. They were pretty good facsimiles of the American variety and very satisfying. We didn't talk while we ate, and I had a chance to observe my young friend. She was eating with gusto and showing no signs of a concussion. My relief after days of worry and searching was overwhelming, but now that I had Courtney safely under my protection, I realized that I had a lot of questions that I wanted to ask. Annoyance at all the trouble she had caused was beginning to gain ground over my relief.

"Are you feeling better?" I asked to get the conversation going.

Courtney nodded but then gave an almost imperceptible shiver.

"You know that your mother has been beside herself with worry."

Courtney looked blank. Then, unexpectedly, she began to sob quietly.

"Okay, okay," I said, softening. "It's all right. You're with me now, and we'll call your mom as soon as we pull ourselves together."

She kept sobbing and shivering, and I got her my hooded sweatshirt and draped it around her, trying to calm her down.

"Courtney," I said quietly, "you're safe now. Really. You know that I'm a private investigator that your mother hired to find you." I took out my P.I. card with my picture on it to reassure her. "Your friends, the two Jessicas at Madeira, tipped me off about your going to Oaxaca, and then I met Ramon, and found a part of your matchbook collection down in a tomb at Monte Alban." I showed her the matches from J. Gilbert's and she sobbed more loudly. She was getting all runny and really starting to blubber.

"But, Courtney, it's all right now. Calm down and we'll call your mother and get you home."

Courtney sobbed louder. I led her to the couch and put my arm around her.

"Your mother will be so relieved to see you. Shhh. Shhh. I remember when I was about ten years old and I ran away one summer to the farthest part of the seashore that we could see. I remember crossing jetties and piers, and swimming laps, and climbing slippery rocks, and finally I reached it. But then I knew that I was too tired to get all the way back, and I was scared and cold, and the sun was beginning to go down, and I just wanted to be home. And, you know? My parents had sent my older cousin, Alan, to come find me, and he did and got me home. That's why I'm here for you."

Courtney had continued to sob, paying scant attention to my soothing story. Finally, she blurted out, "You don't understand at all. Someone tried to kill me." I had guessed that much. She paused. "And, and—Ramon is d-d-dead." The last word came out in a fit of sobs.

"What? Are you sure he isn't just—um—asleep?"

"He's dead. I found him there. It wasn't supposed to work like this. It got all wrong. I don't know what to do."

"Courtney, you're going to have to explain all of this to me. But first—" I thought quickly; I needed a plan. My first duty was to my client and the safety of her daughter. But Ramon dead? I couldn't believe it. I had to see for myself. "Let's call your mother and let her know that you're safe," I said. "Then I'll call my office and have someone come down here and take you home."

This sensible plan seemed to elicit greater wailing and more waterworks. "I can't go home. My mother would kill me. And she'd be right," she added with a few more sputterings.

I sighed and closed my eyes. "Okay," I said. "Let me call the office and they'll call your mom."

"Please don't leave me here," Courtney said.

"Of course not. Here. Take this," I said, belatedly finding my little travel pack of tissues. "Now splash some water on your face, and we'll figure out how to place a call from the room."

Courtney reluctantly went into the bathroom, and I heard the heartening gush of plentifully running water. I knew that there was a lot more to this story than I had figured, and I was worried about Courtney and Ramon and who knows what else.

Courtney came out of the bathroom looking pale but calmer. We sat down on one of the beds and worked out how to call the U.S. This was certainly better than calling from the front desk of the Hotel Casa Paradiso with Mario torn between listening to our conversation and having to miss some of the finer plot points on the *Zorro* reruns.

I dialed the many digits for the Will Thompson Detective Agency and this time got Michael. I briefly told him that I had found Courtney. "But, Michael," I said, "there's a lot going on down here. And I was wondering if you would have time to come down and take Courtney back. I may have a little more to do here."

"What sorts of things, Schaef?" Michael asked with interest.

"I can't really talk now, Michael. Can you call Mrs. Crawford and tell her that Courtney is safe and then meet us at the Oaxaca airport the earliest flight tomorrow morning? I'll book a flight back for all three of us, just in case I don't have to stay."

"Done and done," he said slowly with some concern. "Marna can handle the office for a day or so. Just hang in there, okay?"

"Right," I said. "And Will? Any change in his condition?"

"No. Not really," Michael said. "I'm looking forward to seeing you both tomorrow. And in one piece. Just lie low till I get there, okay?"

"Okay," I said, managing a smile for Courtney. I hung up the phone. "All taken care of. You leave for home tomorrow afternoon at the latest." With that I called the airline and made reservations for three on the afternoon flight to Mexico City connecting to Dulles. If I could clear up the Ramon mess, maybe I would be on the flight, too. I knew that Courtney was in danger and didn't yet know from whom, but I couldn't just leave Ramon there either.

After making these travel arrangements, my next order of business was a major debriefing of Courtney. Should we do it here or on the way to Monte Alban to check out Courtney's story about Ramon? I thought it extremely unlikely that Ramon was dead and much more probable that he had passed out from an overdose of hashish and Zapotec zeal. But maybe he needed help. Finally I decided that I needed to go back to the Hotel Casa Paradiso to pick up some of my gear and, since I wasn't letting Courtney out of my sight, she would have to go with me.

Our surprise entrance at the Casa was not lost on Mario or the Professor, who were chatting at the front desk. But since I had paid up Courtney's bill, Mario had no reason to be hostile and greeted us politely. The Professor seemed eager to share this new development with others, and, after some charming salutations, excused himself quickly. At least Rosa did not seem to be there.

So Courtney and I went up to my room together. We got jackets; I changed my sandals for sensible shoes. I took my small first aid kit, a flashlight, and my spray can of mace. I also took my little camera with light-sensitive film and my night-viewing goggles. I felt a little foolish with all this gear, but I knew that I might need it. In fact, I was already wishing that I had qualified to carry a gun. Nearly everyone in Virginia had one but me.

"Okay, Courtney. We'll walk to the Zocalo and get a taxi. You can start talking any time."

As we walked out of the Casa Paradiso onto the quiet streets, Courtney seemed to wrestle with what version of events she would tell me. I was beginning to get impatient.

"Courtney, fun's fun and all that—" my father loved that expression, "but I think you should tell me what's going on."

Silence. Clicking of sandals on pavement.

"All right," I said. "Start with why you're here in Oaxaca."

"I came to meet someone."

"Uh-huh?" I encouraged.

"Do I have to tell you this?"

"I think it would be best."

"All right," she muttered. "But do you have to tell my mother?"

"No. Not if it isn't strictly necessary. She just wants to see you safe and at home. Courtney, do you think you're in danger now?"

"Yeah," she said.

"And I can protect you better if I knew who hit you and tied you up."

"I know that."

"Well then, spill," I said sharply. "Whom did you come to meet?" More silence. Then:

"Montgomery," she said quietly.

"Montgomery-Crawford-your-stepfather?" I said as if it were one word. I couldn't keep the shock and disapproval out of my voice.

"Uh-huh," she said. "I'm not proud of it."

"Well, good," I said. "There's a start." I sighed again. Now I knew why poor Emily Crawford was looped most of the time.

"You see, he and I have so much in common. We both like to ski and have adventures. Mom is so boring."

"Right," I said, trying to sound noncommittal. "But why did you meet here?"

"Well," she paused again. "Montgomery works in Mexican and Central American trade, and he heard through his contacts that there was an enormous pile of money in Oaxaca. It was sort of a hidden fund made up of contributions from Mexicans over the last few years."

"Whose money was it?"

"I really don't know. Some revolutionary groups, I think. Ramon was part of it."

"Let me get this straight. Montgomery was trying to steal the secret, hard-earned savings of Mexican workers and farmers?" I was both outraged and astounded. Wouldn't it have been easier to tap into the drug trade? Or maybe this was less dangerous. I took a deep breath and continued. "Okay. So what was your part in all this?"

"Well, Montgomery had a contact who gave me a note in code that had half of the information about where the money was hidden. His contact couldn't come, 'cause he was kind of on the outs with this group and really couldn't show his face here. So I was supposed to come to Oaxaca and get Ramon—somehow or other—to give me the rest of the code, and then Montgomery would meet me, and we'd find the money and go somewhere to live together far away. Maybe Tahiti," she added wistfully.

This was truly disgusting. "And what about your mother, Courtney?" I couldn't help siding with the older and wronged woman.

"Well, she had all the money she needed, and Montgomery didn't love her."

"Then what about the people who had collected that money?"

Silence from Courtney. Silence from me. This was the most disgusting story I had heard maybe ever, betraying every good human emotion for the twin motivations of lust and greed.

"Okay. So what happened? What went wrong?" I asked, vowing not to moralize until later.

"Well," said Courtney sullenly, "I tried to get Ramon to like me, and he *did* like me, but Ramon didn't trust me and wouldn't give me his part of the code. I went back last night to try again. And that's when I found him."

"Found him?"

"You know," she paused. "Dead."

"And?"

"And I got really scared and knew who you were because Ramon told me and where you were and that you were looking for me, so I started back to try to find you, but it was dark and someone came up from behind and hit me on the head." It all came out in one long breath.

"Is Montgomery here in Oaxaca?"

"I...don't know. I haven't seen him."

"But you suspect he's here? Why? Have you talked with him?"

"Well, I did talk with him yesterday by phone. He had given me a number to call, but I wasn't sure where it was."

"Was it local?"

"Uh, yeah. I guess it was. He told me to throw the number away afterwards."

"Well, what did he say?"

"I told him that I thought I was making progress with Ramon, but that he hadn't trusted me with the code yet. He told me to try again. He tried to pretend he was patient, but I could tell he was stressed out and really upset. He said something about running out of time. He ended up by swearing at me," she concluded sadly.

"For goodness sake, Courtney, how did you get into this mess?" I regretted the words as soon as they were out of my mouth. "Oh, never mind. I've done some stupid things in my day." First, there were husbands one and two. Then there was Oaxaca.

We got to the Zocalo, which was well lighted and bristling with activity. I noticed Marjorie and the Professor at one of the little tables on the east side cafe/bar. The Professor raised his coffee cup in a gallant salute. Marjorie looked hard at my new companion and me. Good gravy, I thought. This town was smaller than McLean.

24

Night of the Dead

IT WAS GETTING TO BE DUSK by the time we had crossed the Zocalo and located the taxi stand. There were two taxis at the stand, and I negotiated with the driver of the first one. His name was Pedro, and he appeared shocked that we Señoritas wanted to see Monte Alban after closing.

"Pedro," I said, "it will be a big fare. You could drive us up, wait for us, and drive us down again. You could keep the meter running the whole time."

Pedro looked put out, checked his watch, and shook his head sadly. But he agreed to the gig, and off we went. The car, an early-model Chevrolet, climbed the road to Monte Alban with difficulty.

The sunset on the mountain was magnificent. Courtney and I were quiet along the way, each, I think, engaged in our separate thoughts. I had a lot of things to think about, including the lurking and menacing presence of Montgomery (he hadn't seemed so menacing at lunch, only unreliable); the possibility of having to use first aid on Ramon; the really offbeat story about the hidden stash of money; and the necessity of getting Courtney home in one piece. Courtney was no doubt meditating on the folly of love and the disgrace of betrayal, but her face looked impassive. Pedro's inner life was outside of my ken.

After about 20 minutes of grinding gear changes and hairpin turns, we reached the top. I made Pedro promise to wait (not paying him as an incentive), and Courtney and I got out.

It was awfully quiet on the mountaintop, and stars were beginning to spread against the pale sky. A rising moon illuminated the great pyramids and grassy spaces. I felt both awe and low-level terror.

Courtney and I both knew the way through the break in the barbed wire; I got only a few savage scratches on my arms as I clambered through. We both knew the way to the entrance of the tomb where we had both last seen Ramon. Silently, we made our way to the hidden steps leading to it. I got out my concentrated-beam flashlight, pushed aside the bushes, and began to walk down the steps, keeping my left hand on the now damp walls.

"Courtney," I whispered, "hold onto my belt so that we don't get separated."

I felt the awful sense that we were not alone, but I put this down to the miscellaneous scuttling and slithering sounds as we descended the stairs. I groped along trying to find my way to the larger chamber, but it was difficult in the narrow labyrinthine passages. Several times we found ourselves at a dead end, staring blankly at a solid stone wall. I swallowed down the panic. Courtney followed dutifully, holding onto my belt, but completely passive, like a dead weight. I wasn't sure that she wanted to arrive.

"Courtney," I hissed, "you have to help out here. You've been here before by yourself."

"Uh, okay," she said dubiously. Courtney took the lead, and I took the precaution of keeping my left hand always on the left wall, a trick for getting through labyrinths that I had learned from—was it husband one or two? By that method, although you might be dead of old age by the time you arrived at the center, it was logically impossible not to arrive at all.

Courtney proved to be a pretty good guide, though, and after a few false turns we arrived in the same anteroom of about eight feet by twelve feet in which I had gone with Ramon one night before. I used my flashlight to find the candleholder that Ramon used to light the room, and lit the many candles with my matches. The candles illuminated the room somewhat, flickering in a draft and casting grotesque shadows on the walls.

It seemed to be true. There was Ramon, sprawled on the floor in his Zapotec clothes. He certainly looked very still. Courtney and I walked up to him slowly, and I noted the ceremonial knife that I had seen in Ramon's hands last night lying next to him. Reluctantly, I picked up Ramon's left hand and felt for a pulse. Nothing. I pulled out my compact and held it up to his mouth for breath. No mist. As I looked more closely, I saw that Ramon's neck had been slit with a knife in one clean cut. A pool of blood had formed on the ground, covered mostly by the plumes of his headdress. I looked at Courtney, and she looked at me, and neither of us had to say anything.

I got out my camera and opened the F-stop as wide as I could. I took pictures as I had been trained to do from many angles, including from above the body. I took long shots showing Ramon's position within the room.

I searched the room quickly using the quadrant strategy. There seemed to be little there. Some hashish equipment, candles; a ceremonial statue that I remembered from last night was lying on the ground, shattered. Chinks of rock had been removed from the wall and smashed on the ground. If I had had to guess, I would say that there had not been a struggle. That Ramon either knew his assailant or was too drugged out to care. But there were signs of a search.

I got out my fingerprint kit and collected some from the obvious surfaces. The knife handle, the metal in Ramon's intricately patterned designed breastplate, and his headdress. I put a tiny piece of the shattered statue in a plastic bag as well. Was there something I had forgotten?

"Courtney," I whispered, in deference to the dead and to the place. "When you came here last night and found Ramon, did you touch anything?"

"Well, yeah. Of course," she talked quickly. "I bent over him and I think I may have picked up the knife… I'm almost sure I did."

"Oh, God," I sighed to myself. What a time to display curiosity. "Never mind," I said out loud. "The police will get the person who did this." I tried to sound businesslike. "I guess there's nothing left to do here."

Courtney looked stunned and nodded. Just then we heard a noise from above our heads.

"Let's go," I said. We left immediately, trying to retrace our path, but in our hurry making wrong turns, stubbing toes, and scraping our arms on jutting stones. I heard another noise that didn't sound like a lizard. With Courtney clutching my belt, we moved on till we saw the flashlight catching the green of the bushes at the entrance of the tomb. As we were making our way back to the barbed wire opening of the site, walking across the great plaza, I thought I caught a glimpse of white linen, just behind one of the stone slabs with the carvings of warriors. I had a fleeting thought that that was La Llorona, but I didn't let on to Courtney. She'd had a hard day already.

It was about 10:00 when we found Pedro leaning on his cab and smoking an ill-smelling fag end. He pointed with annoyance to his watch and jumped into his seat without any pleasantries. Courtney was near comatose in the back seat and we rode back to the Zocalo in silence.

25

The First Part of the Puzzle

I HAD TO ADMIT that I was shaken by finding Ramon dead. Oh, I had seen a few dead folks before, in apprenticing with the Will Thompson Detective Agency. Some were a lot bloodier. Some even smelled bad. But this, for Heaven's sake, was someone I knew, someone I had been with just hours before. It was a cliché to say that he'd been so alive. But dammit, he had been. A womanizer maybe; a fanatic, certainly. But it was truly awful to see him lifeless and still.

As if in mocking contrast, the Zocalo was brimming with activity, lights, music, and festivity, although it was about 10:30 when Courtney and I arrived in Oaxaca Central. McLean would have been about dead by this time. Maybe a few cars at the Silver Diner, but not much going on outside the discrete and separate suburban houses with their secrets and their silences.

Besides lamenting Ramon's death, I had been doing some hard thinking on the cab ride back, and I had decided that it was time for another debriefing. With determination, I put the corpse out of my mind.

"Courtney," I touched her arm and brought her out of a trance-like state, "I think we need sustenance. I'm buying." I ushered her across the square to my favorite eating establishment where they served the great beef tacos and beer. I ordered a platter and a beer for each of us. We sat at a small table outside. The air was still warm and sweet. I checked for familiar faces and saw none, and when the food came, I waited until we had both had a good share. Then I began the second round of questioning.

"What I'm wondering right now is, can you show me your half of the message?"

"I can't do that," said Courtney.

"You can't do that," I echoed wearily.

"Well, I gave it to someone for safekeeping. I didn't want to give it to Ramon until he was ready to give me his half."

"Do you mind," I asked courteously, "if I inquire as to whom you entrusted this message?"

Courtney hesitated. I gave her my most withering look.

"Okay, okay. I gave it to the Professor. You know, from the Hotel Casa Paradiso. He seems so reliable."

"I guess." "Reliable" would be about the last adjective to come to my mind. "Did you read it first? Do you remember what it said?"

"Of course I do." She was offended.

"Well?"

"It said...something about Bill and Tom meeting in the morning."

"Who are Bill and Tom?" I asked, thoroughly baffled.

"I don't really know. Like, I think that there may not be anyone with these names. It's part of a code. Or their code names."

"Well, we've got to get the paper back." I paused. "You didn't tell the Professor what this was all about, did you?" I remembered his desperately impoverished state plastered over with the sheerest veneer of education and respectability. A great pot of money would surely look awfully good to him.

"Well, not really," she mumbled. "I don't think so," she corrected herself. "Not all of it, anyway," she concluded dejectedly.

Well, this was really great. The code, or at least part of it, was with the Nutty Professor and possibly Marjorie by this time. If the Professor ever fell off the wagon (and I wasn't at all sure that this wasn't a daily occurrence), he might say anything to anyone.

Courtney and I ate ravenously and drank up. I left a lot of pesos on the table and told Courtney that we were on our way to find the Professor. Of course we went first to his usual cafe bar on the east side of the Zocalo. I scanned the tables, but he wasn't there. Desperate, I went up to one of the waiters and asked in broken Spanish, "Donde es el Profesore?" I tried English next and got results: a shrug of the shoulders. "Por favor, please, es importante." The waiter must have sensed my urgency. "Es posible, que esta en 'La Nublina Roja.'"

"Muy gracias, muy gracias," I thanked him.

"Courtney," I said sternly, "do you know where this Nublina Roja is?"

"Sure. It means Red Fog. I can take you."

With no hesitation, Courtney led me down a side street out of the east side of the Zocalo. We walked down the dark side street until we came to a red blinking neon sign—"La Nublina Roja—Funkiest Disco Dancing." The North had evidently brought its cultural advantages to its good neighbor to the South.

Around the entrance was huddled a group of men, apparently the "unable to pay" crowd. Either the light was dim or they all looked menacing.

"Ay, mi vida, mi amor, bella Señoritas. Pay my way and we dance all night," said one, putting his face close to mine.

"Dios mio," said another to Courtney. "You need a handsome hombre to go with that face. Could you lend me some dinero?"

I looked straight ahead, marching Courtney beside me and hoping that if we didn't acknowledge their presence, they would melt away. We walked down some stone steps into what seemed to be a rabbit warren. I could see nothing but smoke. But apparently the place was densely inhabited. Dark shadows were seated at tables while more dark shadows were vibrating on a dance floor. "Stayin' alive, hah, hah, hah, hah, Stayin' alive"—the noise assaulted my ears. Strobe lights bounced off the wall, fluorescent speakers pulsated, and over all the smell of marijuana was thick and sickly sweet.

The Mexicans had given us the Dance Folklorico, and we had given them this.

Perspiring, I stood there. How could we find the Professor in that darkness? Determined, I finally pushed our way up to the bar, where I shouted to the bartender, "Donde es el Profesore?"

"Ahh." He pointed south and disappeared into the murkiness.

I groped in the general direction indicated, holding onto Courtney. Finally I saw a man in a general state of collapse, his head resting on the table. Could this inhabitant of Gorki's *Lower Depths* be the Professor? He looked like a medical specimen in the last throes of liver degeneration.

"Professor?"

No answer.

"Professor, please. I need to speak with you." I shook him, at first gently and then more vigorously. Finally, he raised his head and looked at me. His eyes were bloodshot, his mouth was slack, and the remains of a fried egg were nestled in his beard.

"Please, Professor. We need to talk."

"Hello." His voice was pitifully weak. It was obvious that he needed a transfusion of some kind.

"Are you all right? Would you like something?"

"Yes, I'd like—" The effort was too great, and his head fell into his hands.

"How about some coffee?"

"That's not..." he closed his eyes. "Not exactly what I had in mind. I was thinking more along the lines of a straight tequila. Yes, that's it." He pretended to think over a myriad of possibilities and then select this one. "A tequila would do it. Yes, that's exactly what I need."

His head fell upon his breast. I had to do something. "Just a minute, Professor." I looked around for a waiter. No one fitting that description could be found. Only undulating skintight jeans advertising Calvin Klein,

Guess, Gap. "Just a minute," I said in desperation. "Courtney, sit here and do not move. I'll go to the bar and get a drink."

I had to push and shove my way through the crowd. A man, with his shirt open to his naval, stepped in my path, his arms stretched out, palms up. "Quiere boogie, Senorita?" I pushed him away and fought my way to the bar.

"Please," I said with the urgency of someone calling for a life raft, "a double tequila!"

"Gotcha," said the bartender, who seemed to be a refugee from Forty-Second Street, and winked at me. "One double coming up."

With the drink in my hand, sloshing about, I started to fight my way back to our table. "Wanna deal, baby?" whispered a seductive Latin voice in my ear. I ignored him and kept going. When I finally got back to our table, the Professor was, if not in a robust state of health, at least operative. He was contentedly savoring a drink, oblivious to the relentless beat of the music. Like an old magician carefully testing the results of some mysterious potion, he sipped his liquor.

When he saw me with the drink in my hand, he said, "Thanks, my dear. That will do nicely for later. While I was waiting for you, I managed to procure a tequila from a kind and considerate handmaiden who was hovering nearby."

"Courtney?" I looked at her, and she shrugged with a glimmer of a smile.

"I will survive, I will survive, heh, heh," exploded the music. My temples were throbbing.

"Please, Professor, can we talk now?"

The Professor just hummed and smiled. "No hurry. 'The bird of youth is on the wing,' the poet says. 'Drink to the bird.'" He raised high his glass and drank. "No hurry."

"Professor," I pleaded, "how about some food? Or black coffee?"

"Schaeffer," the Professor looked at me impishly, "if you give coffee to a drunk, all you've got is a wide-awake drunk."

I looked stricken.

"Oh, all right." The Professor slowly started to disengage himself from his chair. Then he sat down again. "But first we must clear up the little matter of our bill." He snapped his fingers. "Mozo !"

Immediately, the youth I had seen earlier materialized and handed me a piece of paper closely covered with numbers that looked roughly like the Lybian defense budget.

I started to protest, but when the waiter said, "What's the matter? You think I cheat you?" I quickly said, "Oh, no. I was just adding up the tax." He still looked steely-eyed. "And figuring out the tip," I added. His stern expression relaxed into a smile. I handed over 25 pesos to the waiter. "The Red Fog" may have been tawdry, but it certainly wasn't cheap.

"Come on, Courtney, Professor. Let's go."

But there was no response. The Professor just sat there in a catatonic trance.

"All right," I said to Courtney. "Help me put him on his feet. We've got to get out of here and dry him out." Courtney was probably used to this anyway. What with her mother and all.

Together we lifted him. It was like raising 150 pounds of wet laundry. But between us, we managed to walk him out of the disco.

We dragged his inert form along and finally came to a bench in the park. No one was around. The family parties had all dispersed, and the park looked beautiful under the bright stars.

"Let's set him down here on a bench," I said. "He'll come to after awhile." But he didn't. And I couldn't think of a way to get him home. Finally, after an hour, a taxi cruised by. It was Pedro. But Pedro was reluctant. His light was off, he protested. He wanted to go home to his wife and his bed—and besides, the borracho señor might dirty his Chevrolet cab.

Finally, after much persuasion, Pedro drove us to the Professor's van, where the three of us got him into the vehicle and maneuvered him onto a small cot covered with newspapers. The van proved to be a hodge-podge of candy wrappers, books, and old bottles of hair dye. I could understand the candy wrappers, but I hadn't known the Professor was so concerned with his appearance. It was a mess—something like the descriptions of the homes of the elderly who live alone amid dirt and squalor and are later found to have squirreled away millions. The squalor was there, but I doubted that he would turn out to have a lot of money.

I looked at the Professor and the surrounding mess. "This isn't going to be any fun, Courtney, but we've got to find the piece of paper."

"Before Montgomery does?" she asked shakily.

I looked at her carefully. It was clear to me that she was beginning to question what side Montgomery was on and who her real friends were.

"It probably wouldn't hurt," I said noncommittally. "What sort of paper was it, anyway? White, small, wrinkled, what?"

"Well, it was white and just a thin strip like it was torn off a larger sheet of paper. The writing was black pen, I think."

"Excellent," I said. "Now get to work."

Amidst the clutter, the books, periodicals, paperbacks, and empty tequila bottles, this could be tough.

"Courtney, you start at the door and work toward me. I'm going to do the heroic work of searching the Professor's person." I thought it was likely that the Professor would be carrying his note in a safe place somewhere in his clothes. Still, he could have squirreled it away somewhere in the debris of his living quarters.

Putting aside my distaste at the assorted smells of old sweat, tequila, and whatever else, I started at his head and felt first around the blue paisley scarf he affected at his throat. Nothing. I then reached into the pocket of the frayed white shirt with button-down collar. Nothing but a tattered membership in the American Association of Retired Persons.

Next were the pockets of his tweed jacket. Nothing but a few pathetic pesos and some Chiclets—bought from a Oaxacan child to cover tequila breath? The Professor moaned slightly and turned on his side.

All right, I said to myself. I will have to reach into the Professor's pants pockets. If he wakes up now, he'll think I was coming on to him. I could never show my face in the Zocalo again. Well, bitez le bullet. I reached in. In his right pocket, I felt a leather wallet. Wishing I were wearing latex gloves, I inched it out carefully. It was brown, frayed, spotted and worn but looked hand-tooled, handsome in its way, sort of like the Professor.

Inside the billfold were 100 pesos (so he could have paid his own bar tab, I thought with annoyance) and a folded white strip of paper about one third torn off from an 8-1/2 x 11 piece of typing paper. I unfolded it carefully and read. "See Tom. Bill'll come too."

"Courtney," I called softly. "I think I've found it—the 'Tom and Bill' note. Is this it?"

Courtney hurried over and looked at it. "Yes," she said, "I think that's it."

"Good," I said. "Hasta la vista, Professor," and I led Courtney quickly out of the trailer.

26

Breaking the Code

WHEN COURTNEY and I got back to the Hotel Casa Paradiso, Mario was still up, watching the flickering lights on the TV. He nodded at me and gave Courtney a quick once-over. Since I had paid her previous hotel bill, I guess that Mario was willing to let bygones be bygones.

I greeted him quickly and asked if I could have a cot put into my room for Courtney.

"One hundred pesos extra per day," he asked.

"Absolutely," I agreed, and we all three headed up to my room, each carrying a part of the bed or bedding.

Courtney and I slept for nine hours straight. But when I woke up the next morning, I was not refreshed. Foggy of mind and flannel-mouthed, I roused Courtney and we went down to have the usual coffee grounds and evaporated milk the hotel called "Cafe Americano." She was bleary-eyed and still shaky and would not leave my side.

Astoundingly, we saw the Professor sitting at a table in the hotel breakfast room, in a little alcove conveniently near the kitchen where Carmen, the chef, waitress and maitre d', was boiling water and charring toast. Through the open door, you could not only give your order but also watch it burn.

"How are you, Professor?" I said curtly.

"Excellent. How should I be?"

And indeed he did seem well, exceptionally well. His dark eyes were bright, his skin baby-pink, and his voice had lost its quaver.

This really annoyed me since I was feeling terrible without having had the fun of a prior orgy. "I'm glad you're feeling fine *now*," I said, hoping at least to get a thank-you for my efforts on his behalf.

"'Come live with me and be my love,'" he called, "or at least come over to my table and sit with me."

"Later," I mumbled, nodding toward Courtney. Had the Professor noticed the loss of his precious scrap of paper? Impossible to say.

"Buenos dias, buenos dias." Mario came over to our table bristling with excitement. I looked at him. "Did you hear the terrible thing that happened?" Mario's eyes were shining with that special look of someone coming to impart bad news, especially sanguinary bad news.

"What—what happened?" I asked. Was this more bad news or just what we already knew?

"Lo mataron. Murder." Mario paused dramatically to savor our first shock.

"Anyone we know?" asked the Professor calmly.

"Yesterday the body of Ramon Gonzalez was found by guards in one of the ruins at Monte Alban—hacked to pieces by a machete!" Now Mario's eyes were positively glistening. "His beautiful black hair was all thick with blood." And now Mario leaned closer to me. "And his ears and—er—private members were shredded! Ramon smelled," he stopped and held his nose, "he smelled of death and rottenness."

My stomach lurched. Courtney turned very pale. Was this mutilation true or was it mere embellishment?

"But who could have done it?" I said quickly, trying to look shocked.

"We are not sure. We are not even sure when he was killed. We think the body had been lying there for two days."

That clearly was embellishment. "But who wanted to kill him?" I asked again.

"Many women," Mario leered. "We think it was a crime of passion.

Poor Ramon had many amores. Right now the police have in custody Rosa because she was found hiding nearby."

"Rosa? That's impossible," I said.

"Perhaps," put in the Professor. "But Rosa may have been pregnant, you know. As they say, 'Hell hath no fury like a woman spermed.'"

We all stared at the Professor with distaste.

"Rosa," said Mario, "has sworn on her tono that if she couldn't have Ramon, no other woman could."

So Rosa *had* followed me back to Monte Alban after all. She had to have been there when Courtney and I were checking Ramon's body. And I had seen the white presence. Rosa must have been La Llarona after all.

But had she killed Ramon? Or mutilated his body? Or just had the bad luck to be caught there? And had she hit Courtney over the head, bound and gagged her, and left her to die? I just couldn't believe it.

"Rosa Calderon is a fine person," I said aloud. "I can't believe that she would have killed Ramon." I remembered uneasily my suggestion to her that it might be the *man* and not the other woman who needed to be punished. Perhaps she was only half-convinced and decided to punish both.

Mario shrugged. "The police put Rosa into custody. I will arrange for a lawyer, of course. She is known in the community and also needs to return to her village to help with the weaving of rugs."

Courtney and I excused ourselves quickly and went back up to my room. I had to think out our next move.

First, I thought about checking out of the Hotel Casa Paradiso, even if I were going to stay on for a few days. I estimated that Courtney and I were in considerable danger from Montgomery, who would want his scrap of paper back, and possibly even from Rosa, who would be out on bail or on her own recognizance soon. But Oaxaca was such a small town. Would changing hotels really protect us? In the end, I decided to wait for Michael, who was due in later this morning.

Courtney had been pretty nearly silent since getting up. "Schaeffer," she finally said. "Do you think it's true—about Ramon being hacked up and all?"

"I've been thinking about it myself," I said. "And I really don't know. But I do know this. When my colleague gets here, we're getting you out of Oaxaca."

"But I can't go home," she began to stammer. "And I don't think that I'm safe anywhere. I'd just as soon be killed here and not have to face my friends."

Was this clarity of thought or self-pity?

"Why do you think someone wants to kill you?"

"Because I have the note with half the code," she said. "And I think Montgomery was just using me. I think..." she trailed off. That way madness lay.

"Okay. Here's what we'll do while we're waiting. Let's work on the code and see what we can make of it—"

"But it's only *half*," Courtney interrupted.

"Nevertheless," I replied firmly. "And let's get my roll of film developed. I want to have a record of how we found Ramon last night."

With that plan of action, I got out the folded piece of paper and spread it carefully on the bed. I snapped the window shade down so that we could have some privacy, and turned on the single overhead bulb. We stared again at the now-familiar words: "See Tom. Bill'll come, too."

"Are you sure that you don't know who Tom and/or Bill are?" I prompted.

"No," said Courtney impatiently. "I told you it was in *code*."

"Right. The words are arranged in an awfully funny way. You know, we need to look at this with a fresh point of view. Sort of like crossword puzzles. Let's not try to think of these as words, but just letters, or even shapes. Rid your mind of preconceptions."

Courtney gave me a disgusted look at my New Age riff, but she looked at the words as though she was trying to make them out.

It struck us both at the same moment. "Tomb," we both said at nearly the same time. And indeed, detached from their meaning in the sentences, the letters spelled out "Tom. B."

Then I had a second flash: the "i" and the four "l's" added up to 5. That is, Tomb V at Monte Alban!

I shared this insight with Courtney, who wasn't impressed. "But Tomb V is where I went with Ramon. It's where he always hung out. I know that place. Ramon knew it. You searched it yourself. There's no treasure there."

I had to agree with Courtney's reasoning. Either the treasure was never there or someone had taken it before killing Ramon. But maybe the other half of the code was there! That might not be so conspicuous as a treasure. Had Ramon had it or not? I ran through my search of Tomb V in my mind. Had I done it thoroughly? By the book? I thought so.

"Okay," I said, vastly deflated. We had come so far, gone to all that trouble to find the scrap of paper. We had even decoded it and what did we have to show for it, but a dead end. It was a little like looking for Tomb V last night and suddenly coming up against a stone wall. Scary, in-your-face, and seemingly final.

Not only had we reached a dead end, but Rosa was possibly homicidal, Montgomery was on the loose and desperate, Ramon was dead, and Courtney was in danger of being next.

"Let's get out of here," I concluded. We packed our few things, and we made our way downstairs.

We stopped to drop off my film at a photo shop in the Zocalo. I figured that the pictures might tell us something that we had overlooked. And it would also be a record of how we found Ramon.

Then we went out by taxi to the Oaxaca airport. I had booked three flights—one way—back to Dulles International Airport in McLean,

Virginia, for later that afternoon, just in case I decided to return as well. There was nothing left to do but sit at the airport and wait for Michael's plane to arrive. Reinforcements were beginning to sound pretty good.

27

Puerto Escondido

ANIMA SOLA is a Mexican term used to denote a wandering soul, a person who had died alone and has no resting place. Sitting in the small open airport that morning, I felt that that was me for sure. No one would come and place wreaths at my graveside on the Day of the Dead; no one would bring my favorite flowers (daisies); or my favorite foods (bread, butter, and bitter hot chocolate); or mourn me when I was gone. Man, was I feeling sorry for myself.

Michael was the third one off the plane at 10:00 that carried about eight people. You know what it's like when you've missed someone an awful lot and not even known how much? You see someone as if for the first time. In a cartoon, your eyes would pop out and go "boinning!" I felt that way now. Michael was about six feet tall and a bit on the portly side. Not fat, but always working to make sure that his stomach would not protrude too far over his belt. His appeal lay perhaps in his strawberry-blond hair that he kept relatively short, but which fell over his forehead. His eyebrows and eyelashes were the same color, and his fair skin was covered with freckles. I liked the way his brows knitted together in concentration. I liked his upturned nose and wide smile. I don't know; I was just glad to see him. What did it matter that he seemed interested in me one day and not the next, and that he was in a long-term relationship to boot? He walked quickly to us, and put down his bag. I gave him a hug and felt, as I had before, that his bear-like body made mine feel very small and delicate. It felt good to be held by Michael. Would I have been just as glad to see Marna and be enveloped in her motherly embrace? I think not.

I then introduced Michael to Courtney and she looked at him with anxiety. She wanted to know how her mother was. Michael assured here that her mother was fine and greatly relieved to know that Courtney was well and on her way home. Also her mother had said that her sister, Aunt Amber, was coming over to stay with her right away.

"Chah, right," said Courtney. "Aunt Amber lives in Akron."

("And she eats apples" I couldn't help finishing to myself. I was feeling more chipper already.)

"Some detective you are," Courtney continued, with a laugh that I was glad to see. Michael looked chagrined but added, "Besides, your housekeeper was there and planning to spend the night."

After these brief introductions, I went to the counter to confirm our flights out in the afternoon. I still hadn't finally decided to go back, but I was beginning to persuade myself that the unfinished business with Montgomery did not need my personal attention. After all, I had found Courtney and was bringing her back. That's what I had agreed to do.

I was dismayed to learn then that the afternoon flights out of Oaxaca had been canceled. Why? Weather. Weather where? I looked out at the clear blue sky around me. The answer was a shrug. Defeated, I booked three seats on the next available flight out of Oaxaca, which would leave at 11:45 the next morning. I broke the news to the others. Courtney was particularly upset. She didn't want to go back to Oaxaca.

Suddenly, I had an inspiration. We could drive to Puerto Escondido, a resort on the coast, due west of Oaxaca. I had read about it in my guidebook. We could spend the night and come back in time to catch the plane. Michael and Courtney were agreeable. We took our bags and climbed into the first taxi in the line of two.

"Where are you going?" said the driver in very good English.

"Could you take us to Puerto Escondido?" I asked.

"Okay," he said, "if I can bring you back, too."

"Absolutely," I said. "We can spend the night—I'll pay, and then can we go back early tomorrow morning?"

"All right," he said and named an outrageous-sounding sum in pesos, which was only about 100 dollars.

"But first can we stop in Oaxaca?"

I needed to pick up my pictures of Ramon and the scene of the crime, and our driver, whose name was Jesus Montoya, (his first name pronounced "hay-ZOOS") needed to call home to say that he would be gone all night. Meanwhile, Michael called Courtney's mother to explain about the delay and offer reassurances.

"'Puerto Escondido' means 'hidden port,'" I told the others as we were finally on our way. "We could use a little cover."

The road started out bumpy and windy, but the cab was pretty nice and had some degree of air conditioning, amplified greatly by a strategic opening of windows. Along the way, I asked about Will. He seemed awfully far away. I could almost not remember how he looked or how I felt about him. Michael reported no change except that sometimes he would say "her husband" as he had before. I guess that Will had come to the same conclusion about Montgomery before we had.

We told Michael everything that we knew and showed him the pictures of Ramon lying dead. He had no comment, though I thought he ought to have complimented me on the quality of the pictures taken at very low light with no tripod. He puzzled with us over the code for Tomb V and asked for assurances that we had searched it thoroughly. We were able to assure him.

"Okay," he said finally. "Montgomery is probably still here and may have accomplices. We have half of the code. Montgomery seems desperate and may be a murderer. I'd say that leaving Oaxaca is a very good idea."

"Yes, but why should we be safer in Puerto Escondido, or McLean, or anywhere else?" Courtney asked impatiently. "As long as Montgomery thinks that I have the code."

There really wasn't a good answer to that one.

Nonetheless, the taxi kept bumping westward. At about nine miles outside of Oaxaca, Jesus stopped the car at an enormous tree.

"This tree," said Jesus, "is nearly three thousand years old." We got out and circled its enormous gnarled trunk. Deciding that looking like tourists on a holiday was safest, I got out my handy guidebook and read: "This famous Tula tree is thought to be the oldest in Mexico. Under its shadow, Cortez is said to have rested on his way to Honduras. With a circumference of 57.9 meters, it is thought to be the thickest tree on earth."

Courtney had trouble with the 3,000 years concept. It wasn't in her frame of reference, to say nothing of Cortez or Honduras. Michael, ever the lapsed Catholic, explained it with reference to Christ's birth. This helped a little. I am the sort of romantic traveler who loves the idea of things that ancient peoples had touched and that I could touch as well. So I touched the trunk gently, relished the shade, and headed back to the taxi.

I was actually a little alarmed at how much English Jesus seemed to know. Could he have followed our extensive discussion of Ramon's murder? He said nothing, however. His next stop was at the town of Tlacolula, where market day was beginning to wind down.

We got out and stretched our legs. We made an unlikely group: Me, a small, blondish, wavy-haired woman; Courtney, a thin surly teenager; and Michael, a tall, massive, freckled, fresh-faced fellow looking about 35. For what possible reason could we three have been thrown together to go on a vacation? It would have seemed ridiculous to another American. But to a Mexican, all of us Americans must have seemed ridiculous anyway.

Jesus suggested that we have something to eat at his friend Juan's cafe, and we agreed. Fortified by delicious bean- and chicken-filled enchiladas and strong coffee, we four wandered back through the market towards Jesus' taxi.

The market, in the fading sunlight, was beautiful, so lovely that you could almost forget the poverty behind the brilliant colors and profusion of unsold goods. We walked through the booths, fascinated. Colors were everywhere: garnet roses, emerald cucumbers, and ruby chilies. Each vendor had made an elegant design of his offerings.

One unbelievably old-looking woman was sitting cross-legged on the ground. Spread out on a large sheet of brown paper beside her were small heaps of hazelnuts and peanuts, surrounded by pyramids of mangoes, here and there graced by bunches of bananas.

Even the gelatin-pudding salesman, standing nearby, displayed his bright-red and chartreuse Jell-Os and yellow flans in a tempting manner—although I was sure that even one bite would bring on a fatal attack of turista. Next to him, a boy of about 14 had arranged candies in a checkerboard pattern on a folding table.

Jesus seemed to know what I was thinking. "It is beautiful, yes, but these people get only a few pesos for their trouble. They can barely live."

I felt ashamed of my largely aesthetic response and bought some bananas for us, some caramels, and a large bouquet of red roses. (I decided to let the gelatin pudding go.)

On the next table were the most endearing tin ornaments in many shapes. I bought one shaped like a cow to add to my cow collection and a tin pig ornament for Will.

Next, we came to a table of curved knives of all different sizes and designs. "These are machetes," said Jesus. "Everyone who works in the fields has one."

"Do you?" I asked curiously.

"Mine is a very small one." From his back pocket he took out a knife and showed it to me. I took it and tried to translate the words on the hilt.

Jesus helped me: "I am a friend of the just, but a scourge of the wicked." I stared hard at him and handed it back, hilt first.

"Perhaps I ought to buy one."

I picked up a pearl-handled one, from which Jesus translated the inscription, "Ay, my little sweetheart—do not use me to destroy our love." I laughed, paid the asking price, and put it in my handbag. The inscription was a little off, but it might come in handy.

We walked on past a booth where a heavily wrinkled woman was selling aromatic herbs. I watched her gnarled hands handing a young woman a bouquet of rosemary and cress, possibly a love token, possibly an amulet against misfortune. She gave instructions in a smothered voice and fell back into an attitude of waiting.

"Superstition," said Jesus unexpectedly. "That is our curse."

I knew what he meant: that superstition was an enemy to real action in overcoming this numbing poverty. But I stopped anyway and asked humbly for a bouquet/amulet for myself. Like a minor character in a Grimm's fairy tale, I was collecting all of the magic and practical tools that I might need on the quest ahead. And I was trying to assuage my conscience by helping in a small, small way to aid the sad Mexican economy. Finally, my arms laden with goods, Jesus and I joined the others at the taxi and drove on.

The road, which wasn't bad at all, took us through undeveloped countryside, then a town so sad and poor that it seemed to be inhabited only by mangy dogs. Nearer the coast we saw clusters of thatched huts looking uninhabited. Our first glimpse of the Pacific Coast was spectacular. I did feel like Cortes, silent on a peak in Darien from Keats's poem "On First Seeing the Pacific." The vast expanse of blue led up to by lovely tan sand and palm trees was truly magnificent.

On closer inspection this "Hidden Port" wasn't really so hidden anymore. Large boxy hotels were plentiful, although there were still hammocks on the beach for nightly rental. I asked Jesus what he recommended, and he suggested one of the interchangeable boxy hotels, called Hotel Virginia, of all places, on Camino Alfaro. Jesus seemed to have a lot of friends, but he claimed not to know the owner of this one. It was simply one that he had heard about. My guidebook confirmed that it had large rooms, large beds, and was very well scrubbed.

We drove up and parked. There were surprisingly few cars about. We walked into the small and antiseptic-looking lobby, and I thought briefly about the lodging situation. Money (since it was Courtney's mother paying, ultimately) was no object. I asked for a single room for Jesus, with an ocean view. Then, I had a small pow-wow with Michael and Courtney. None of us wanted to sleep alone. So I ordered a room with a king size bed and an ocean view and tried hard not to blush too badly. I really didn't want to think about what the hotel proprietor was thinking, let alone Jesus. Heck, maybe I should have asked him to join us. We agreed to meet for dinner in a few hours and to ask for a wake-up call at 5 a.m. We did not want to miss our flight.

28

Blue Margarita

IT WAS ONE of those suspended moments, out of time, out of the trajectory of this sad and sordid story of greed and betrayal. If we were in danger, we didn't feel it, but felt only the moment, marooned in time, in a lovely if impoverished place with hours to fill before we met Jesus for dinner and then more hours till we met our plane for home in the morning.

Seeing the beautiful blue and vast Pacific, Courtney wanted to swim and so did I. Michael was less eager, not having brought the proper gear, but we persuaded him that we wouldn't laugh even if his underwear sported hearts or Bugs Bunnies. Fortunately, the gift/convenience shop downstairs sold bathing suits, which Michael purchased, and rubber flip-flops, which we all bought, to defend ourselves against the spiky sea urchins in the area.

We ventured onto the beach, wide and sandy, graced with palm trees, hammocks, beach blankets, and drink stands. We rented a blanket and towels and lay down to warm ourselves in the late-afternoon sun. Courtney was tanned and smooth in her small blue bikini. Michael and I were a trifle pale and self-conscious, he in his new blue rather brief shorts, and me in a black tank suit that I always brought with me. But the sun did warm us, melted away our worries, and loosened our limbs. I taught Michael and Courtney my favorite mantra from the medieval abbess, Julian of Norwich: "All shall be well, and all shall be well, and all manner of things shall be well." We chanted ourselves into a calm semi-sleep until

Courtney got bored and threw some water on us. Then she grabbed a hand of each of us and dragged us, laughing, into the ocean.

To my surprise, the Pacific here was deliciously warm. In my past, ocean water came in three temperatures: cold (my childhood summer haunts on the Connecticut shore); really cold (one summer's visit to Bar Harbor, Maine); and unexpectedly cold (a public beach between Los Angeles and Malibu). But this water went with what I guessed was meant by a tropical paradise—water warm enough to swim in, play in, and linger in without hurrying out to preserve blood flow.

In this new context Courtney became pleasingly less adult, leading us in swimming heats; a game of grab someone else's legs and try to pull him or her under the water; and body surfing, which kept ending in the three of us crashing against the shore in a heap, our hair full of sand and pebbles.

Finally, panting and sticky with salt water and sand, we threw ourselves back on the beach blanket. All this brought memories flooding back to me of the endless summers my family spent in my grandfather's cottage at the aforementioned Connecticut shore. I shared some of these memories of what now seemed an idyllic time with Michael and Courtney: I told them how we had learned to dive off a rickety jetty, first step-jumping from pole to pole, slippery with algae, then shivering in the stiff sea breeze till our turn to jump in; how our lips would get blue with cold in the Atlantic water and how our mothers would order us—protesting through chattering teeth that we were perfectly all right—out of the water to stand with our backs against the sea wall, which had soaked up sun and warmed us quickly. How we "mined" iron ore in the sand with dime-store magnets, silver in the middle and red on the ends, and "sold" it to our parents. How the Good Humor ice cream truck came by once a week, and we ran up the steps from the beach, with 25 cents grasped in our outstretched hands, eager to devour the blessed Chocolate Eclair on a stick. How the all-family cook-out on the beach on Labor Day, to mark the end of the summer and the return to school, was always the saddest day of my life, redeemed only a little by the hot dogs and roasted marshmallows. Cold was so cold then, hot dogs so salty, marshmallows so sweet.

Courtney had her memories of summer, too. They were mostly summers at Hilton Head, South Carolina, where she was sent yearly to be with Aunt Amber. There one golfed till one dropped, or biked miles across the flat shoreline, and always ended up dressing for dinner at the country club.

Michael had some funny memories of swimming in North Dakota. He hadn't even seen an ocean until he was 25. There was only a swimming hole at his uncle's farm where he learned to swim a little. Later in high school, kids went there to smoke cigarettes and drink beer. The lake near his house in rural Fargo had bad memories for him. It was where his father had made him go rabbit hunting one fall and how, trying to miss a mother rabbit, Michael had accidentally shot Peter Cottontail. This was his last hunting trip, he said. It wasn't easy growing up without hunting in Fargo, North Dakota, and when his parents moved to Arizona several years back, he decided that he would never go back to Fargo again. Mostly, anyway, the lake froze over, and—though he couldn't skate because of weak ankles—he did participate in the yearly betting on when exactly an old pick-up, driven out onto the ice in the dead of winter, would break through the ice, signaling spring.

I noted that rural folks like him sure knew how to have a good time, and Michael retaliated by rubbing sand in my back. I liked that and teased him some more about the average number of pick-up trucks surrounding a typical Fargo, North Dakota, house.

We were all feeling pretty mellow as the sun began to set. A few of our fellow beachgoers, perhaps renegades from Key West, cheered when the sun finally crashed magnificently into the Pacific with a show of orange and yellow and violet and gold.

The sunset brought me back to reality, though. We had promised to meet Jesus for dinner at the rooftop restaurant of our hotel. We got up, kind of stiff with salt and sand, and headed back to the hotel somewhat subdued in the twilight.

We all serially rinsed off in the room's shower in the white all-American bathroom and dressed in the best of what we had with us for dinner. Courtney really looked lovely and not older than her age for once in a pinkish halter-top and loose white pants. I wore a white tee shirt, my least dirty jeans, and platform sandals. Michael wore his usual Brooks Brothers stuff, white shirt, khakis, loafers. I guess Midwestern boys needed an Eastern way to dress that was foolproof and easy to master.

Jesus was waiting for us, looking showered and refreshed. He told us that he had slept after the long drive and then walked on the beach for a while before getting ready for dinner. He looked handsome in a white shirt and black pants, his black hair slicked back from the shower. Courtney looked her usual tanned self, and Michael and I looked merrily flushed from our unusual exposure to sun, water, and frolic.

We let Jesus order for all of us, and he ordered fresh sea bass, rice, and beans. I insisted on each of us having what the menu called their Blue Margarita. The Blue Margarita claimed on the menu to be the specialty of the house. Its ingredients were listed as tequila, lime juice, Cointreau, and a secret ingredient. I was a Blue Margarita virgin, and I wanted my first time to be special.

My first sip of the justifiably touted drink was pretty much a peak life experience. The glass was enormous and blue, with a clear stem and a green base. My lower lip touched the salt on the side of the rim of the glass at the same time that an intense, sweet, limey, potent liquid slid into my mouth. The two tastes meshed and exploded. I didn't know whether the liquid was blue or just the glass, but it certainly tasted blue. I tried it again with similar effect. A few more sips and I would soon be a danger to myself and others.

I may have been wrong, but I thought that all four of us were having a wonderful out-of-time experience. The patio restaurant was lovely, with lights strung on the walls, purple bougainvillea-like flowers here and there, and a lovely soft breeze drifting in from the ocean. Our dinners were wonderful. It was if we had never eaten such fresh fish, such tasty rice, such fulfilling beans ever before. No one complained about the drinks either. I knew that this was a special night for all of us. As if by silent agreement, we allowed no thoughts of work or worry to enter the conversation.

We took turns making toasts as we sipped our margaritas. Jesus started with a traditional Mexican toast, that I did not quite understand, but we all drank to it.

Courtney came up with, "You know, Toto, there's no place like home." We all laughed and raised our glasses.

Michael couldn't come up with a North Dakotan toast and simply said, "Skol!"

Finally, I quoted the song from *Twelfth Night* in my somewhat maudlin, inebriated state: "Journeys end in lovers' meetings, every wise man's son doth know." They all stared at me, ready to be delighted but somewhat understandably baffled.

I tried again. "To journey's end," I said with more simplicity. "To journey's end," they echoed, and we all quaffed our remaining magic blue liquid.

After dinner, we made plans to meet in the lobby at 5 a.m. We left requests for wakeup calls, proposed to set our various alarm clocks, and vowed not to oversleep. We needed to be back at the Oaxaca airport for the 11:45 plane. Our lives depended on it.

Jesus said goodnight and let himself into his room. We three went into the room adjacent (I still wondered what Jesus was thinking) and we took turns in the bathroom getting ready for bed. The room was boxy and square, all white with three colorful Mexican prints on the wall, of the sea, a garden, and a church. There was also a chair and a couch a little too short for comfortable sleeping. The balmy patio air wafted in through the open balcony doors. The bed, thank heavens, was enormous.

To be honest, I was fighting a feeling that I had known was lurking and even occasionally making an appearance since I had met Michael, now almost a year ago. I was badly attracted to him. Badly, inappropriately, hopelessly. Intuitive as he was, he must have understood this—maybe even from the first night that we met, when Will, Michael and Marna had to tell me how they had discovered Nick in the hotel room with Roger from Accounting. I reddened when I remembered how Michael had perhaps in effect been warning me that night when he told me that he had a live-in lover. He had told me that before he ended the evening with what was, for me, an unforgettable momentary but deep connection in the form of a long, close hug.

How vulnerable I had been that night. Well, I was a little less so now. I could keep my feelings hidden and well under control in any case. I had once asked Michael to describe his long committed relationship with Anna, from the World Bank. "Flatline," he had said. When he looked at my horrified expression, he added, laughing, "In a good way. Rock solid." Would I ever be able to say that about a committed companion of mine?

It was indeed a strange pajama party. Courtney got into bed on the far left side, quickly fell asleep, and started to snore in a ladylike manner. I got in next to her and lay on my back. I was forming a chaperone-like buffer and trying hard to keep my limbs from touching anyone on either side. Michael jumped in on the far right, grabbing the sheets and the light blanket. His relative bulk produced a deep indentation on his side of the bed and set off a chain reaction, causing Courtney to roll into me and me into Michael. I gently pushed Courtney back to her side, gingerly moved back to the middle, and suddenly started to giggle. So did Michael. We tried to shush ourselves but couldn't stop. I think it was the first time that we had really laughed since Will's shooting. Or maybe it was the Blue Margaritas.

When we finally got silent, Michael put his arm under my shoulders and I rested my head in the crook between his neck and well-padded chest.

"It's been pretty grueling for you, Schaef," he said. "Glad you're coming back with me tomorrow."

"Why did you do that, Michael?" I asked.

"Do what?" he said, not moving.

"The arm," I whispered. "Under my head. Are you being avuncular or making a move?" I had to know because I wasn't feeling niece-like or whatever the counterpart to avuncular is. I felt a rush of warmth. The same rush I had felt during our first hug but more so.

"I'm not sure," Michael said, and then he turned and kissed me.

It was like tasting the Blue Margarita at dinner. There was salt and sweetness and intense pleasure. A few more sips and I would be a danger to myself and others.

"Michael," I murmured. "What about Anna?" (And what about my buried feelings for Will? I asked myself simultaneously.)

"Please don't ask me hard questions, Schaef," he said quietly. "Things have been a little rough between me and Anna lately."

"Is that your final answer?" I said. "Or do you want to phone a friend?"

"My final answer," he laughed. He kissed me again, deeply, and wrapped his arms around me, holding me close to him. Then he gently traced the small bones of my back. They felt delicate against his strong hands.

Next to us, Courtney began to stir.

We untangled ourselves slowly and quietly. We kissed one more time.

"I guess I'll be sleeping on the couch tonight," Michael said in his sweet reedy voice. "To be continued," he added and took his pillow over to the couch.

Lying alone with Courtney, I felt acutely the absence of his warmth. I sighed. No telling where this journey would end.

I had to say my Julian of Norwich mantra over and over before I finally fell asleep.

29

The Second Half of the Puzzle

THE NEXT MORNING at 4:30 a.m., bells seemed to jangle all at once. The hotel desk called, two travel alarms went off, and Jesus knocked on the door. I leapt out of bed, let Jesus in, and got first dibs on the bathroom. I was glad that Jesus had got a chance to see Michael sleeping on the couch just in case he had feared the worst.

As I dressed, I remembered last night. What had it meant anyhow?

Fortunately, our hurry was good camouflage for any awkwardness between Michael and me. We all made it downstairs in record time, where mercifully there was a large thermos of coffee with packages of sugar and non-dairy creamer. I quaffed two cups with the thirst of a desert traveler. I certainly hoped that Jesus was feeling less hung over than I was.

Fortunately, Jesus seemed to have the trip well in hand as we raced over the bad roads and good roads, retracing our steps as the sun came up in front of us all rosy-fingered and peach and yellow.

I opined as how I much preferred sunsets, no matter how extravagant and colorful the sunrise was. This opinion was greeted with sleepy murmurs from Michael and Courtney in the back seat.

In fact, I was beginning to feel a little more alive than dead, and, as Jesus concentrated on his driving mission, and Michael and Courtney dozed in the rear, I had time to collect my thoughts and feelings.

My first thought was how much I missed Michael already; his warmth and his sweetness mingled with the always-inexplicable animal attraction

I felt for him. What had happened last night? Something real or just "a moment in the woods," a midsummer night's dream that would vanish—in his case at least—in the clear light of day? As for me, yes, I was drawn to Michael, but was he simply a safe embodiment of the unattainable, or did I really like him? Or was I so overwhelmingly drawn to him now because he represented safety, help, and home?

Another thought assailed me then. Could I really go home with Michael and Courtney? I didn't really think that my new friend, Rosa Calderon, was a murderer. Montgomery Crawford, lost, with no way back, had to be the one. Would any of us be safe with Montgomery Crawford trying to find us and find out what we knew? Yes, I had found my client's missing daughter, but was she as good as dead, even in suburban McLean, if I couldn't find Montgomery as well? And if I did find him, what then? If he had killed Ramon, how could I prove it and get Montgomery behind bars? I really didn't have any answers to those last questions. Maybe the secret would be to get rid of our half of the code. It was useless to us and a source of danger at the same time.

"Ahem," I said loudly in Michael's direction. "I need to discuss an important case with you."

Michael roused himself and sleepily rubbed his eyes in an engaging childlike way. "Okay," he said. "What up?"

"Michael, I think that we need to get rid of our half of the code so that we won't be in danger."

"But we know the code even if we aren't holding it, so we can't not be in danger, if you know what I mean."

I knew exactly what he meant. I had just been indulging in wishful thinking. "Well," I said, "How can we keep Courtney safe then? I'm worried that she won't be safe even at home." Michael looked thoughtful and didn't answer.

Just at that moment, Jesus swerved off the road and parked in front of a small roadside cafe. Jesus had needed a short break, and he ordered coffee and last night's tortillas for all of us. We sat in a small garden off the side of the cafe and drank our coffee silently.

"You know those pictures of Ramon's body?" Michael said suddenly. "Maybe we overlooked something. You know the book I gave you when you passed your P.I. exam? On steganography? That's hiding things in plain view," he explained to Jesus and Courtney. "Let's look at the photos again with fresh eyes. Montgomery thought that Ramon held the key to the coded message. Maybe he did and didn't let you or Montgomery know."

I thought fondly of Michael's gift to me. I had read the book cover to cover, lingering often on the sweet inscription: "To a fellow P.I. May all be revealed." I knew it by heart. But snapping myself out of my daze, I got out my envelope of pictures that I had taken of the crime scene in Tomb V at Monte Alban. I hated to look at Ramon, but I had to admire how thorough and professional my photography had been. We passed the pictures slowly among us and studied each one carefully. I looked at Michael, Jesus, and Courtney in turn. Was there anything here that we hadn't seen?

Suddenly, Jesus laughed out loud. "His breastplate!" he said. "The patterns are the patterns at Mitla."

"Mitla?" we all repeated stupidly.

Mitla, Jesus explained patiently, was the second most famous archaeological site near Oaxaca, after Monte Alban. It was mainly the burial site of the same Zapotec civilization, but its buildings and tombs were marked with very distinctive zigzag repeating patterns, somewhat Greek in appearance, which made up the patterns on Ramon's ceremonial breastplate.

We all drew the obvious conclusion at the same time. The treasure wasn't hidden in Tomb V at Monte Alban as we had all assumed. It was hidden in Tomb V at Mitla. It had to be. Ramon had known the code all along but had died rather than reveal it to people whom he could not trust.

"Jesus," I said slowly, wanting to be sure. "You said that there are tombs at Mitla? Say, for example, at least five?"

"Of course," said Jesus. "Mitla is most of all a burial ground. There are more than five tombs."

We stared at each other and then at the bloody pictures of Ramon with his intricate breastplate. No one said a word.

Finally, Michael looked at his watch and startled us all with a nasty expletive. "We've really got to get to the airport or we'll miss the plane back. We need to get Courtney out of here."

I fished out some pesos to cover our breakfast and a good tip, and we gathered ourselves up and got back in the car. Jesus and I again sat in the front and, fueled up on coffee, Jesus really began to race. Nobody dozed but nobody talked either, and I had some more time to mull over the current state of affairs.

You see, I was deciding—no, I *had* decided—that I wasn't getting on the plane to Virginia with Michael and Courtney. Oh, part of me wanted to go back somewhere familiar, to my little yellow cottage. I wanted to have a familiar American Christmas with snow and department stores looking all festive and smelling so great, and visiting the National Christmas tree, with all of the 50 little state trees around it. I wanted to be home where Michael might kiss me again and where we might begin to unravel what had happened between us and maybe to knit it back together again.

But part of me wanted to stay in Oaxaca and find the treasure and somehow neutralize Montgomery. I was proud of the work I had done, and I wanted to finish it. It was partly wanting to keep Courtney safe, and it was partly pride of workmanship. I wanted—no, I needed—to finish this case.

As we neared the airport, I decided on a dramatic scene on the tarmac with the propellers turning, a la *Casablanca*. I thought that this would be better than a whiny and protracted discussion in the car, a la 'You should go with Courtney and I'll stay here,' or 'We could both bring Courtney home and then come back' and so on and so forth. In such a situation, I would probably lose my resolve.

Instead, as I planned, we all got out of the car at the tiny, open-sided terminal, where we could see the plane for McLean, Virginia, ready for boarding. Courtney and Michael got their suitcases out of the trunk, but I took mine out and left it in the back seat.

"You know, Michael, that I need to stay here and finish this, don't you?" I said. To his credit, he didn't argue or discuss.

He gave me a long look. "All right, " he said. "I'll be sure to get Courtney home safely."

He smiled at me. "You'll keep in touch?"

"Like I want to be left all alone with no lifelines?"

I think that he might have wanted to say something about the night before, but maybe he was relieved that he didn't have to. "All right, my fellow P.I.," he said. "May all be revealed." Then he gave me a quick squeeze and walked off toward the plane.

I hugged Courtney then and wished her a safe journey. She looked sad and to raise her spirits, I added, "We had some excitement, right? Lots to tell our grandchildren. .." Courtney was starting to tear up. "Hey," I said. "It will be all right. Give my best to the two Jessicas and be good to your mother! She loves you, you know."

Courtney didn't want to let go. I understood that she was not looking forward to facing her mother. But in a moment she straightened up and, with a healthy sign of grit, muttered, "Get that Montgomery bastard for me, Schaef," and she, too, walked to the plane.

Jesus and I were left standing on the tarmac. I had an irresistible urge to say, 'Jesus, this could be the start of a beautiful friendship,' but I quashed the impulse. Instead, I turned to him and asked, "Are you ready for a little trip to Mitla?"

30

Reality Check

I SHOULD PROBABLY say a few words about Jesus at this point. First of all, he was incredibly smart. After all, it was he who (at least we hoped) had solved the second half of the code, Tomb V at Mitla, not at Monte Alban. But, in addition, he seemed really nice. A fine person. The kind of man you could trust with your secrets and with your life. Not really the kind of person you would want to lead into danger if you had a choice.

I told you that he was smallish, dark, and compact. He had looked very handsome the night before in his clean white shirt and black pants. Today he was in his more traditional outfit of a salmon shirt and matching salmon fake-leather jacket. He also wore black-rimmed rather thick glasses for driving. These made him look sort of Woody Allen-ish, but in a nice way, as though Woody Allen were both very smart and very sweet.

Now, when I asked him if he would take me to Mitla, he looked down at the ground and thought a bit. He knew, of course, that this wasn't going to be your average tourist taxi ride. He knew what he was becoming a part of and that I (certainly) and he (quite possibly) could be in a lot of danger from a man who had already killed once for what we were trying to find. As he looked down, I guessed that he was weighing the odds and thinking about where his commitments lay.

After what seemed a long time, he said, "I'll take you. But first I will stop home and tell my wife where I'll be."

We drove to the outskirts of Oaxaca and stopped at a medium-sized apartment building. Although I wanted to wait in the cab so as not to intrude, Jesus insisted that I come in—to be out of harm's way. I yielded finally and we walked up two flights of stairs. Jesus let us in with his key, and his wife, Dolores, came out and greeted him with great warmth and concern. While embracing, they spoke rapidly in Spanish. Dolores was sweet and lovely, a perfect match for Jesus, it seemed. When she understood who I was and why I was there, she brought me into the living room/dining room/kitchen/nursery and insisted that I take coffee and a sweet roll, which was delicious.

At that point, Baby Alexandro toddled in and Dolores picked him up and began to nurse him. He seemed a little old for this by American standards, but I understood that this was the custom in Mexico. Then she seated Alexandro in a high chair and offered him Cheerios, which he chased around his high chair table with one sticky finger, occasionally putting one in his mouth and chewing it contentedly. Some behaviors are apparently universal.

I talked about how cute Alexandro was and how grateful I was for her husband's help. I could tell that she was trying hard not to resent me as she moved about the kitchen part of the room, packing a lunch for Jesus and me. I didn't know how to reassure her in my very weak Spanish.

In a few minutes, Jesus came out, embraced Dolores and little Alexandro, and spoke rapidly to them in Spanish. I shook hands with Dolores. She managed a smile. "I will be home for supper," Jesus said reassuringly, and we left.

Somehow meeting Jesus' family, however briefly, gave me a heavy dose of reality. I was single. No one would miss me much, but Jesus was important to at least two other important people. I felt bad about getting him mixed up in my North American sordid detective mess. Just because he was smart, kind, a good driver, and used nearly perfect English was no reason to get him into mortal trouble. Quite the contrary.

"Jesus," I said as we got back into his taxi and started off on the road to Mitla, "I really appreciate all that you've done for me. And I don't want to put you in any danger. Dolores and Alexandro need you a lot more than I do." He smiled and drove on.

"So first, I want to pay you for yesterday's trip, and today's trip, and—if you're right about Tomb V—for solving the code to the treasure." I handed him a large number of pesos, enough I hoped to do him some real good and to put away something for the future. I could afford to be generous, I thought. Emily Crawford would never even miss this amount. It would just cover one more trip to Vail, Colorado, and after the events of the last month, I'd bet that she would never want to see that particular place again. For Jesus, on the other hand, I hoped it would be a nest egg.

Jesus took the bills with a simple "thank you" and didn't try to count them. I liked him even more. I decided then that we ought to stop so that I could get in the back seat.

"When we get to Mitla, I'm going to look around Tomb V as inconspicuously as I can. Just blending in with the tourists. I'm going to give myself one hour—find anything or not—and I'd be grateful if you would wait for me by your cab. That's what you would usually do, right?"

"That is right."

"At the end of one hour, I'll want you to take me back to Oaxaca. Then we say good-bye, Okay? I don't want you more mixed up in this than you already are."

"Okay," Jesus said. I'm glad that he knew where his priorities lay. My staying in Oaxaca was my own doing and I had no right to endanger someone else, let alone someone like Jesus.

"But if I don't make it back to your taxi in one hour," I went on, "I want you to leave without me and drive back to Oaxaca. Then from a pay phone, call the police station and tell Detective Mestas where I am. But you've got to stay anonymous." I figured that Detective Mestas, the policeman that Archie Hayes had led me to when I had first come into town, would be interested in the disappearance of yet another nordamericana.

The trip took us about 45 minutes. When we arrived, it was anticlimactic. The village of Mitla itself was barren—just one large parking lot. Jesus told me that the town had a lovely inn that I could see from the road. It was charming, built in Spanish Colonial style. Mitla also had a church and a small museum, the museum maintained by the archaeology department of the University of Oaxaca. And of course Mitla had the ruins and the tombs.

What really concerned me at this point was where Montgomery was. Why hadn't I seen him? I had been taught to spot a tail. And working with Will, Michael, and Marna, I had even learned to feel the presence of someone following me. Thus far I had not. I knew that Montgomery was in the area because of the phone call to Courtney. If he was not following me, was he still keeping tabs on Courtney? That was almost as disconcerting a thought as his tailing me.

Jesus let me off a short way from the entrance to the ruins and told me that he would be waiting. It was getting on to midday and becoming extremely hot. I tried to keep within the shadows of the bazaars that lined both sides of the street. The sounds, sights and smells from the stands of fruits, flowers, woven blankets and rebozos were in incredibly sharp focus for me. My senses felt keener as I hoped that I was coming to the end of my journey and at the same time felt a sense of impending danger. I looked at my watch. It was nearly noon. I had given myself one hour to find what I was seeking.

31

Mitla

THE MITLA RUINS at first sight seemed disappointingly ordinary. The site was not glorious like Monte Alban, not spread out on a mountaintop, but rather bits of stone on flat land surrounded by chicken wire. But once inside the site, the ruins, long and low, were powerful in their own way. As Jesus had told me and I had confirmed in the guidebook, Mitla translated from the Zapotec as "place of rest." The whole place was really a gravesite for kings, priests, and the nobility, originally built by the Zapotecs in the 12th century. As I entered the ruins of what my map called the first Plaza, the silent buildings seemed indeed like a place of death.

But where was Tomb V?

The site seemed to consist of four major palaces and a number of smaller ones, each conceived as a series of chambers around a central patio open to the west. Slowly I looked around. In the first hall were rows of handsomely proportioned columns, but what stood out most were the stunning mosaic patterns that seemed unique among the ancient buildings I had seen—but identical to the patterns on the breastplate of poor, dead Ramon. The designs were everywhere: a "classic, repeating Greco Key pattern," my book said. The patterns were made of stones cut about four inches in length and then fitted together with such precision that no cement had been needed.

I had just emerged from the first building into the courtyard when I saw that I was not alone. No, it wasn't Montgomery. My relief turned to exasperation, however, when I learned that I was about to bond with a group of North American young men with very white shirts, dark ties, dark pants, and shiny black shoes, who appeared to be missionaries of some kind. There were six of them and they were carefully comparing the layout of the site to a foldout map.

Well, I thought to myself, cover is cover—as long as they don't try to convert me. But no—one young man began to approach.

"Do you know," he said in an unnaturally friendly manner as he pointed to the building I had just come from, "that each one of the one hundred thousand stones in that one mosaic was shaped and placed by hand?"

"Hmm," I said and turned my head. I wanted to nip this friendship in the bud. But he still stood there, smiling, his face unwholesomely pale.

"Have you been down to see the Column of Death?" he asked cheerfully.

"No," I said noncommittally.

"Right there," he said and pointed to some narrow stone steps leading underground. "Don't miss it. In the chamber underneath, there's a stone column. If you throw your arms around this stone column, the distance between your hands tells you how long you've got to live."

In spite of the hot sun, I shivered. Naturally this sort of prediction would please the young missionary. As the anguished souls climbed up out of the tunnel, they would be ripe for thoughts of repentance. At the moment, however, my life span was not something I wanted to think about.

"Do you know if this hall is also a tomb?" I asked politely.

"It sure looks like one—and smells like one, too. If you're down there too long, you can't breathe. The only air is coming from the little opening on the top." He looked down and consulted his map. "Yup, it's actually called Tomb Number V. Can I go with you?"

I tried to appear calm and shook my head. "Thanks for all the good information, though." I said this with what I hoped was finality and took a step around him towards Tomb V. He had really been very helpful, but I needed a little space. I needed to search this tomb by myself, checking in every corner, examining all possible hiding places.

He followed me.

"Please, " I said seriously. "If you don't mind, I'd rather be alone. Besides, I don't believe in organized religion. I'm afraid I'm a heathen." My stupidity was apparent immediately. The word "heathen" was like a red flag to a bull. His pale eyes glistened in eagerness.

"Let me help you down," he said. "You seem so alone and so—"

"So irritated," I finished for him, surprising myself. "I just want to be alone."

He looked at me intently and a little mournfully. Another one that got away. "God bless you," he said as he turned back to his friends.

I waited a minute to make sure that he wasn't going to try again, and then I began to go down the narrow stone steps of the tomb. After about eight shallow steps, I stepped heavily onto the floor of a very small low-ceilinged room—even I had to duck my head—with a large column in the middle. I took out my intensive-beam flashlight and as swiftly as I could did the traditional four-quadrant search. It had served me well. I checked each quadrant, marking my progress by the position of the steps, and found nothing. No loose brick, no hiding place, no cache.

I did the search all over again, this time in concentric circles, leading outward from the column. Still nothing. With my high beam, I searched what I thought was every inch of the tomb, but again I came up blank. I pushed the light button on my watch. It was 20 minutes to one. I had only about a quarter of an hour left. I couldn't believe that my search of Tomb V had come up empty. It wasn't possible. Unless there was a flaw in our thinking. Or unless someone had gotten here first.

I nearly cried as I took one last look around. Slowly I resigned myself to defeat, and gave up. But before climbing back up the steps,

I remembered what my missionary friend had told me about putting my arms around the column in the center. If I didn't do it, I would probably always regret it, like leaving the Trevi Fountain in Rome without throwing a coin in over your shoulder.

I put my arms out and embraced the stone column only too easily. Very little space seemed to remain between my hands. How was the space measured? I wondered. An inch to a year?

As I was thinking this thought, I happened to glance upward. From that particular angle I could see the top of the stone wall of the tomb with its Grecian-looking repeating mosaics. How easy it would be to slip something in between the repeated motifs. My flashlight might have missed it, but I'd be darned if my hand would.

I found a loose rock and balanced on it, reaching my hand up as high as I could, sliding my hand back and forth between each of the patterns one by one. Finally, I felt something. I could hardly believe it. I grasped it and pulled it down. It was small thick envelope, the kind with the circular clasp tied with string.

At that moment I heard someone call out, "Are you there? Are you there?" I quickly put the envelope into my bag.

"Yes," I said shortly. "Where could I go?"

"I'm sorry to intrude." It was the young missionary. He climbed down the steps, his shiny black shoes now covered with dust. "But I was worried. You did sound kind of desperate, and I was afraid you'd try to do something unwise." He placed his hand on my shoulder. "There's so much to live for."

"I'm really all right," I said to him carefully. "I do appreciate your looking out for me, though." He turned around and awkwardly climbed up the steps. I sighed. Was my newfound toughness so implausible? Did I still come across as needing to be cared for? Or was it just a missionary thing?

I looked at my watch again. I had less than seven minutes before 1:00.

Eager as I was to open the envelope, I knew that I had to get back to Jesus and out of Mitla. I was simply too exposed here. I was just about to head back up the stairs when I thought I saw the same dusty shoes descending. There was room for only one on these stairs.

"Good gravy," I said, feeling really exasperated this time. "I asked you to leave me alone!"

But the shoes slowly and inexorably came down the steps. Suddenly I was face to face, not with the missionary, but with, of all people, Archie Hayes.

"For the love of Pete," I said in a terse whisper. "What are you doing here?"

"I might well ask you the same question," he said in his usual Texan drawl. "I work here with the archeology group attached to the Museum. This morning I thought I saw you come down here, and I wondered what new trouble you had gotten into."

Did I buy this seemingly innocuous explanation? I didn't really know what Archie, the ex-Texan, did, only that he seemed to know his way around Oaxaca.

"Oh," I said as offhandedly as I could. "No need for you to worry. I'm just on the regular tourist path doing Mitla this morning."

"Did you ever find your gringa friend?" asked Archie.

"Actually, yes," I said with some hauteur. "But she left for home today." Damn! Why had I said that? Did I need so badly to show off? Who was Archie Hayes anyway? Suddenly I didn't want to be sharing a very small space with him. "Can we get out of here?" I said. "It's a little dank for my tastes, and there's really only air for one."

My annoyance was at myself. I shouldn't let my pride get the better of me. And I shouldn't be giving information to strangers, even helpful ones. A little self-control, please.

"Nice to see you," I continued, as we emerged into the sunlight. "My taxi driver is waiting so..."

"So..." he echoed.

"So I guess I'd better be going," I finished.

We stood there in the hot sun looking at each other closely. It occurred to me that Archie wanted to say something to me, but I couldn't imagine what, and he obviously couldn't imagine how.

"Good-bye, then," I said and turned back toward the exit from the ruins. I tried not to look rushed.

Jesus was waiting for me by his cab. I got into the back seat and he quickly started back on the road to Oaxaca.

"I've got it, Jesus," I said with excitement as we were safely on our way.

32

Treasure

I LOOKED BEHIND US to make sure that no one was following the taxi. It seemed all clear.

"Jesus," I said excitedly, "I found an envelope hidden in the patterned stones in Tomb V, just as you thought I might. I didn't get a chance to open it—if you keep driving, I'll open it right now."

With eager hands, I pulled the envelope out of my bag. It was made of stiff brownish-red cardboard, the kind that accountants use to keep records in, with a tie string around a little round fastener. I unwound the string quickly and opened the top. I stared hard at the contents.

My disappointment was severe. In the envelope, there was no money, no gold, no jewels, no stock certificates, no bank book, no rare stamps or coins—nothing at all like that. I couldn't believe it. There was only a thin sheet of paper, folded and refolded several times.

Near tears of exasperation, I unfolded the paper and smoothed its worn creases carefully. I was expecting, perhaps, another clue, a map, maybe, to the treasure. Something that made sense. Instead, on the paper, in small, meticulous handwriting, was a long list of names, perhaps 500 or more. The heading of the list, underlined twice, was simply "Estas Personas Fideles a la Causa." Even I could understand this. It meant "Those Loyal to Our Cause."

I took a moment to compose myself. It just didn't make sense to me. This was the treasure that Ramon had protected with his life and that Montgomery was willing to kill for?

Slowly, I explained what I had found to Jesus, held up the list, and asked him what he thought it meant.

Jesus said nothing for what seemed like a long time. Finally he said, "These are the names of those we can count on when the time comes to end this oppression."

"'We'?" I asked. "Jesus, is your name on this list?"

Again he was quiet, keeping his eyes on the road. I scanned the names for Jesus's name. There it was, neatly printed, "Jesus Montoya."

I folded the list up carefully and put it back inside the envelope. I was startled and confused. Even though political change seemed to be coming to Mexico, I knew that reform was coming slowly to poor and rural people. I had no doubt that the list was made up of good people, like Jesus, wanting a better life for their children, their families, neighbors, and compatriots. How ironic that Montgomery had killed Ramon for this list of names, which would have been worthless to him. How stupid that Montgomery had destroyed his family in search of a different kind of treasure. And I couldn't believe how bad Montgomery's information had been. Probably from the folks who brought us Iran-Contra or took 14 years to find the Unabomber.

"Jesus," I said after a while, "what should I do with this list? I just want to know what I can do to keep you and the others out of trouble. I don't want this to fall into the wrong hands."

"I think that you should hide the list again. I don't want anyone to know that I know where it is. It would be too dangerous for me." I thought about Dolores and little Alexandro eating his Cheerios and knew what he meant.

"Of course, Jesus. You can drop me at the Zocalo just like you would any tourist and no one will know that you know anything."

"But where will you hide the list? If you put it back where it was,

Montgomery will probably get it." Then he had a thought. "Do you know anyone else on the list?"

"I don't know," I said. "I'll look again." Again I took the envelope out, carefully unfolded the paper, and scanned the names. Unbelievably, I found one that I knew. It was Rosa Calderon's.

As soon as I had found it, I saw that it was obvious. Ramon had brought Rosa into La Causa. She would have done anything for him, anything to be part of his life and his work. Besides, after seeing Rosa's village, I was sure that she would want to help work for a better life.

"Jesus," I said, "I see one name that I know. Would it be safe for you if I told you only the one name? Then I could give the list to this person and this person could be sure that it was in safe keeping until the time was right."

Jesus agreed that it would be good to know one name. I told him Rosa's and the name of her village and also that Rosa had been Ramon's lover.

"I'll get this list to Rosa or die trying," I said.

As we approached the city, each lost in thought, it soon became clear from the crowds and general confusion that something was happening in the Zocalo. Jesus explained that La Noche de Rabaños, the Night of Radishes, was taking place. This was a yearly event near Christmas where Oaxacans carved statues and elaborate tableaux out of radishes. A jury prize of $500 was given to the best one. This seemed highly improbable to me, but I could see, even from the outskirts of town, that it was a great event and that people had come from all over for it, Mexicans and tourists alike. The crowd would certainly make it hard for me to get Rosa, but, on the other hand, it would provide me with a little camouflage.

"We're not far from the center of town, right?" I said. "If you drop me here, I can easily walk to the Hotel Casa Paradiso." He slowed down and pulled over to the curb. "Thank you for everything, Jesus. Please say hello to Dolores and Alexandro, too."

I wanted to linger but I didn't dare. I placed my bag military style across my shoulder and chest, got out of the taxi, and joined the crowd surging towards the Zocalo.

33

Girl Meets Evil

AS I WALKED toward the town square, a rudimentary plan was forming in my now-agitated brain. I had two objectives. I needed to get the list safely to Rosa, and I wanted to bring Montgomery out of the woodwork. But how? Where? By what means? And if I did find him or he found me, what would I do then? Tell him his search had been futile? Get him to confess? Turn him over to the police? I hadn't actually worked out that part yet, and it was getting harder to think clearly, what with all of the noise and festivities.

When I got nearer to the heart of the Zocalo, music came at me from all sides. A band of mariachi musicians played in the white-painted gazebo in the center of the square, and on the other side, a group of Tuña musicians, dressed in dark-red velvet like Spanish nobility, sang Spanish songs. I could see people waiting patiently in a long line to file past what had to be the radish exhibits.

I was just getting my bearings, following alongside the long line when a bony hand reached out and grabbed my shoulder. I turned abruptly around in startle mode and saw the Professor and Marjorie close by, standing in line to see the exhibits.

The Professor was cheerful and charming as ever; Marjorie looked extremely sour. I think that she blamed me in some inexplicable way for Ramon's death. I had felt that she had loved him deeply, protectively.

"Ola, my North American compatriot," the Professor said jauntily.

"We've missed you these past days. The Hotel Casa Paradiso is cheerless and drear without your presence and that of your young friend." I looked skeptical. "'I called for madder music, stronger wine...'" he went on undiscouraged, quoting an obscure Edward Dowson poem, "but to no avail."

Clearly he was flattering me with an end to pumping me for news, information, or even a scrap of dubious gossip. Had he yet realized that Courtney and I had absconded with his coded clue to the whereabouts of the "treasure"? I still couldn't be sure.

"My dear Professor," I said, and nodded solemnly at Marjorie as well. "Courtney and I have simply been seeing the neighboring tourist sites. We were in Puerto Escondido last night and Mitla this morning."

"Breathtaking, both," exclaimed the Professor with disappointment.

At that point, the germ of an idea, perhaps one of the worst I've had, gestated in my brain. Here was my thought: I needed to have Montgomery come find me. Now, in all likelihood, he was following me already, but I suspected that he wouldn't make himself known to me until he was sure that I had found the "treasure" and could be persuaded to hand it over to him. My idea was that, instead of being quiet about it, I would announce my find to the world by means of the two worst gossips in Oaxaca, who now happened to be standing at my elbow. Without thinking it through carefully, I proceeded with my plan.

"But not only did we go sightseeing," I continued in a reckless manner, "Courtney and I actually found what we were looking for. If you know what I mean." The Professor and Marjorie exchanged looks.

"In fact, I have it on my person right now and had better be off to put it in a safe place."

The Professor got a hold of himself. "I hardly know to what you refer... uh, perhaps you could show us?"

"I don't think so, Professor. Not here in this crowd."

"Well then, don't run off. We're nearly at the exhibition now, and when we've finished, we could retire to my trailer for some high tea and a glimpse of what you've found."

"No, really," I said. "I have to be going." Out of the corner of my eye, I had a glimpse of an incredible sight—tableaux carved out of large radishes, as ingenious and detailed as could be imagined. I saw several versions of the Christ child in the manger, the barn complete with horses, sheep, and donkeys. Further down the line, I could just make out some modern-themed sculptures, one depicting the Mexican Revolution and one of the death of Zapata. It was really astounding.

"Good-bye," I called out as I broke free of the Professor's grasp and made my way slowly and conspicuously across the Zocalo.

I paused carefully at several snack stands selling fresh coconut pieces, flan custard, tacos, and candy. I finally decided to buy some packaged caramels. (I knew my life was in danger, but I wasn't crazy.) I tried to enjoy the sunlight and the happy throngs of merrymakers. I then walked slowly through the square, stopping at the gazebo and swaying in time to the mariachi music. I wanted to give Montgomery plenty of time to locate me.

Finally, in the late afternoon, about an hour later, I made sure that my pocketbook was firmly across my chest with the envelope securely in an inner zipped compartment. Then, still facing the musicians, I pulled out my pocket mirror and a lipstick and pointed the mirror carefully above my left and then right shoulders.

At first I saw only what was to be expected. There were festival-goers strolling, children eating sweets and running in circles, and dogs and cats chasing squirrels up trees. And then, catching my breath, I spotted the man that I had last seen at the White House dining room, that I knew to be an adulterer, an almost child molester, a would-be thief, and a murderer. With all about to be exposed, I knew also that the only way that he could disappear was with a lot of money. He had to be desperate for the fortune that he thought I had. Of course, it was Montgomery Crawford.

34

Girl Gets Religion

◗ WHEN I SAW Montgomery in the mirror, he was about 50 feet away from me, just staring at my back as if deciding what to do. No more the jovial, bon vivant denizen of the Old Executive Office Building, the man looked thin, deadly serious, desperate, and very scary. As I looked at him in the mirror, his khaki jacket fell open to reveal a gun holster with a gun—a Smith and Wesson pistol, I think—with enough firepower at close range to put me out of his way for good.

Seeing him and then the gun—well, I'll admit that I simply froze. I never knew before what it meant to be paralyzed with fright. I had thought it was only a metaphor. But suddenly I was. If I had had to make a movement at that moment, I don't believe that I would have been able to.

Guns, per se, didn't frighten me. Will, Michael, and Marna all had registered guns, which they took out occasionally on assignment. But those were guns where they were supposed to be, like in the waist-high holster of policeman in D.C., next to the handcuffs. Montgomery's gun, strapped to his thigh, within easy reach of his right hand, chilled me to the bone. He had the look of a terrorist ready to shoot everyone in the reception area of a government building. But I knew that he was ready to shoot me. The gun itself looked so big, so metallic, so real.

I had never had to contemplate my own death so concretely. Montgomery could simply shoot me and probably even get away with it here in Mexico, where I had no friends and the police had many crimes to solve. I didn't want to be dead. For the first time for a very long time, I knew that clearly. It wasn't that I had so much to live for, but the potential is always there while you're still breathing. Dead, well, it's all over. And I knew suddenly that I just wasn't ready to pack it in.

I told myself that plan A, letting Montgomery find me, was really not working. Indeed, it was a wretched plan. I was alone, outclassed, and outmaneuvered. I needed a plan B and fast. Okay...the new plan of choice, if I could will myself to execute it, was simple. I would get away from Montgomery and find help.

I concentrated. I told myself that if I wanted to live, and secondarily, if I wanted to get the list to Rosa, I would have to conquer this paralyzing fear. I was alone. There was no one there to do it for me. It was just me, myself, and I.

I took a few deep cleansing breaths and put away my lipstick and mirror. Then, without looking back, I began to walk off to the right. I went up the first side street that I came to and then zigzagged up another street. I walked four blocks, each time changing direction. My shoulders felt tense and stiff. My back felt like a target. I expected to feel the sickening rip of a bullet in my back at any minute. I didn't dare turn around to look, but I finally stopped briefly at a street corner and listened, still not looking back.

On the suddenly quiet street, I could hear footsteps behind me and knew that someone was following me. I glanced back and saw that it was Montgomery.

Not pausing again, I ran quickly forward this time and nearly crashed into two men coming in the opposite direction. I grabbed onto the arm of one of the men for safety.

"Help me," I said, trying to catch my breath. "There is a man following me." I looked back and the two men followed my gaze. Of course, there was no one in sight. The men shrugged and pulled away, not understanding.

I started running again and didn't stop until I came to the plaza in front of the grand and famous Church of Santo Domingo. It was twilight and the church was all lighted up as if in anticipation of some special celebration.

Glancing quickly around, I did not see Montgomery, but I found a group of about ten women worshippers dressed in black. I slipped in among the group and we entered the church together. My group of women paused at the massive entrance and crossed themselves. I did as well and quickly scanned the magnificent gold baroque ornamentation of the church, looking for a place to hide. I glanced upward at the ceiling, which was decorated with a Tree of Jesse with seemingly a thousand branches all encrusted with gold. In fact, the whole church was glittering with gold work in the light of many candles. Quickly, I also noted that there was a second-story balcony around the nave but couldn't see any stairs leading up to it.

My group moved forward, as did I, down the spectacularly gilded nave, past many, many rows of handsome wooden pews, across the transept, and reached the main altar. Then the women walked slowly to a chapel to the right of the altar. I walked with them. In the chapel, the women crossed themselves before a statue of St. Bernardo, who was dressed in a red velvet cape and a long white flowing shirt edged with gold. They knelt in the front pews of the chapel. I knelt, too, among them, seeking protection while they sought the solace of prayer. But soon my women began a new ritual, one in which I could not take part without risking exposure as well as blasphemy. In front of the statue of St. Bernardo, amidst the many candles, were a number of vases of tall gladioli flowers. Slowly, in groups of twos and threes, the women went up to the vases and tore off the orange and flame-colored petals. They rubbed the petals first on the feet of the Saint and then on themselves. This I could not do, though heaven knows I felt in need of divine intervention. Instead I sank back in the first row of pews closest to the altar and tried to formulate another escape plan.

With trepidation, I looked back over my shoulder down the long nave. There, in front of the finely carved doors of the entrance to the church, was Montgomery Crawford, clearly looking for me and coming forward toward me on the right side of the pews.

I didn't hesitate. I raced back up the left side of the chapel and into the main church. Again, I scanned my options: out the door into the street, inside a confessional—then I saw a small door in the corner of the nave. I opened it, climbed a steep staircase as fast as I could, and found myself on the balcony of the church. Unfortunately, once up on the balcony, I found that there was nowhere to conceal myself. The interior walls were covered with life-size oil portraits of Saints but no furniture, nooks, or crannies. There was only one exit—the way I had come up.

I tried to flatten myself against the wall, hoping to merge with the picture of St. Catherine carrying her head, but it was useless. If Montgomery had seen me open the side door and disappear, this was the end of the road.

I waited for what seemed to be a long time. Was it possible that I had managed to evade him? If so, I would just stand here until Montgomery had surely given up and had left the church, hoping to find me in the street. I would find a priest and then a policeman, and all manner of things would be well.

A few minutes later, I heard a door open and the stairs begin to creak. I knew then that I had been indulging in wishful thinking. Clearly Montgomery had seen me go in through the door. He was even now climbing the stairs, and would soon be next to me. With his gun. He was at the end of his road, too, and I knew that he wouldn't let me stand in his way.

Suddenly, surprising myself, I stopped cringing. Why should I cower in fear in front of this man? I had a weapon, too. I reached into my bag for my tear gas canister, with Marna's hand-crocheted cover on it. Just at that moment, Montgomery appeared on the balcony, his gun now in his hand in plain view.

I was wrong before. From close range I could see that it was a Smith and Wesson revolver, a .357 Magnum. The gun mesmerized me, sapping my will to fight back. Montgomery was clearly planning on taking no prisoners. He walked toward me and stopped about three feet away.

"I know that you've got it," he said.

"What—what do you want?" I stammered.

"You know goddamned well what I want," he said a little more loudly. "Just give me what you found, and I'll just walk away."

"I don't believe you, " I said, stalling as I found my tear gas canister and maneuvered my thumb onto the trigger. Thank goodness this model was failsafe: it could only be pointed in the right direction. I just needed to get it out of my bag without getting shot. "I think that you killed Ramon for what I have. Why shouldn't you kill me?" I said, trying to keep my voice steady.

Montgomery's patience seemed to be wearing thin. His voice was strained as he aimed the gun at my heart and removed the safety catch. "I said, give it to me NOW."

My hand was still in my pocketbook. Could I get it out and fire the tear gas canister before Montgomery could fire on me? I counted to myself, planning to pull out the canister on "three," and hoping—no, praying—that Montgomery's initial confusion would work in my favor. I put the odds at two to one, in favor of Montgomery.

Just then, when I had counted to "two," a miraculous thing happened. From below on the church floor, a man's voice rang out and echoed loudly, calling out Montgomery's name. "Montgomery Crawford!" the voice shouted out and echoed on the gilded walls of the sanctuary.

For one instant, Montgomery took his eyes off me and looked down to the church floor to see where the voice was coming from. I didn't look or hesitate but pulled my tear gas out and fired it all in Montgomery's direction. He went down, dropping his gun, clawing at his weeping eyes, coughing and choking.

I stooped and grabbed his gun, then ran out past him on the balcony, down the stairs, and through the wooden door to the nave. I closed the door behind me.

As I paused at the wooden door pondering my next move, whom should I see walking up to me but Archie Hayes.

"He's up there?" Archie asked, nodding to the balcony.

I nodded. "I tear-gassed him."

"Are you all right?" he asked.

"I think so," I said. I was suffering some residue of tear gas along with the shock and all.

"Archie," I said, getting my wits together, "who the hell *are* you? How did you know Montgomery's name?"

"Never mind that now," drawled Archie. "He'll be all right in about five minutes. I need to get the po-lice here." He put the accent on the first syllable. Archie took out his cell phone and called the Oaxaca police station. He talked rapidly in Spanish, probably with his good friend Detective Mestas. In about a minute he was off the phone.

"Okey-dokey. The po-lice are on their way. I think that we can keep Montgomery on the other side of that door till they get here, but just in case…" He opened his coat and showed me his gun. Maybe I ought to have taken the gun training after all. I was beginning to feel at a definite disadvantage. I gave Archie Montgomery's gun to add to his collection.

"Archie, before the police come, we have some talking to do. First, who are you?"

"Hey there, little lady," Archie said. "Keep your shirt on. You met Courtney's real father, Curtis Smith, right? You know that he was CIA. I'm his old buddy from those days. When you told him where Courtney was, he called me and asked me to go down and keep an eye on her. He would have gone himself, but he suspected Montgomery would be here and didn't want to tip him off. Besides that, I've worked this territory and know it like the back of my hand."

I was in deep shock and denial, but I didn't have time to sort all that out then. I swallowed my pride. "Thank you for coming in when you did. I think you saved my life."

"Aw, it was nothing."

"When the police get here, can we make sure that they know that Montgomery murdered Ramon? No need to go into motive."

"No problem with that. Once they have Montgomery in custody, there's more than enough to put him in a Mexican lock-up for life. He earned it."

I had to agree.

"Listen, Archie, I know that I'll have to have a long talk with the police and all, and I'm happy to do it, but can you do me one last tremendous favor? There's something I need to do before I talk to them. Can you handle this for about two hours? Then you can find me at the Hotel Casa Paradiso on Alameda. Or if I'm not there, I promise to let you know when I'll be back. I promise I won't run off. I just need to do this."

"You got it, my gringa friend," said Archie.

I smiled at him and walked quickly out of the church. I had my life, my "treasure" intact, and I was off to find Rosa.

35

Farewells

I'LL SPARE YOU the details of my meeting with Rosa. It was a pretty emotional meeting. Thank heavens I found her at the Hotel Casa Paradiso and didn't have to go to the jail or to her village to find her. She had been in custody only one day when her lawyer, provided by Mario, negotiated her release.

I told Rosa the whole story of why Courtney and I were in Oaxaca and everything that had happened since we got here. She, in turn, admitted that on occasion she "became" La Llorona in order to scare off any would-be suitors of Ramon/El Coyote. She also admitted to putting the sugar skulls on my bed for the same reason. (Note to self: find a Spanish-language edition of the self-help book *Women Who Love Too Much* and send it to Rosa. What a classic predicament... I ought to know.)

There were a lot of tears for Ramon, or El Coyote as Rosa still called him, but I was able to comfort her a very little bit by telling her how he had died a brave death fighting for their cause. He had given up no secrets and fought to the end. And I told her that I had seen him dead and that there had been no grisly mutilation as Mario had suggested. I also assured her, and I know that she believed me now, that I had had nothing to do with Ramon in a sexual way and that he had not been interested in me or Courtney at all except as we were political pawns. I didn't really think it necessary to go into Ramon's actions when under the influence of certain illegal substances. He was a good man and his memory did not deserve it.

At the end of an hour, I showed Rosa the list that I had searched so hard for and asked her to keep it safe. I told her that she would know when the time was right to bring the list out of hiding. After more tears and embraces, Rosa accepted the envelope and said that she had to go. I didn't ask her where she was going. I didn't want to know anything about where she would hide the list, though I thought that it would be at her village or maybe at the Hotel Casa Paradiso.

I don't have to say that I admired her courage. She had been brave and ingenious in defense of El Coyote; I believed that she would show the same fortitude and cleverness in carrying on his work.

I then waited for Archie Hayes, who escorted me to the police station, where I was interviewed once again by the dapper and distinguished Detective Mestas. This is where I had started the Mexican leg of my missing person's case; I felt that the wheel was coming full circle.

I told the whole story pretty much, but I never admitted to being a hired private investigator, in case it would land me in a cell next to Montgomery while I waited for my nordeamericana friends to bail me out. Instead, I said that I was asked by Courtney's mother to find her, which I did. In the course of finding Courtney, I explained, I ran afoul of her stepfather Montgomery, who was furious at me for interrupting their sordid domestic drama. Montgomery was also in a jealous rage, I suggested, when he killed Ramon.

With not a cloud on my conscience, I was able to write that out under oath and sign it. Now, what Archie, the ex-CIA man, knew about all this I never really knew and didn't want to find out. But—either as a kindness to me or a courtesy to Courtney's father—he let me say it all without contradiction. And I think that allowing me to go off and finish what I needed to finish before going in for questioning was his way of saying that he would stay out of this affair.

I had to go over my story many times over what seemed like several days, but was really only about an hour. This repetition included detailed accounts of how Montgomery tried to kill me on the balcony of the

Church of San Domingo, which Archie verified for me. Archie corroborated my story by producing Montgomery's gun and my empty tear gas canister, which I had dropped in my haste. Finally, after endless repetitions, Detective Mestas seemed satisfied. Having Archie there helped my credibility a lot, and I owed him another favor. At the end of the interrogation and the signed affidavit, I was told that I could leave Oaxaca. Nay, I was not-so-subtly encouraged to do so. Trouble like me a good tourist season didn't need.

Once again Archie dropped me off at the Hotel Casa Paradiso. I still had many questions for him.

"So you knew who I was from the beginning?"

"Yup."

"And got a seat next to me on the plane?"

"Uh-huh."

"So why didn't you go in and find Courtney and confront Montgomery yourself?"

"Why should I? You were doing a great job. All I had to do was lie low and watch."

There was veiled compliment in there somewhere, which completely took the edge off my annoyance. I'm a sucker for the slightest praise.

"Archie," I said as he dropped me off, "I'm on the 11:00 plane out of Oaxaca the day after tomorrow. You can assure your friend, Detective Mestas, of that. And, you know, I don't think that I'll be heading down this way again. Though, don't get me wrong—the climate is great, the town is charming, and the sites are first rate. It's just, I don't know, Ramon being killed and all. I can't feel the same about it."

Archie nodded.

"But anyway, I've decided to throw a small dinner tomorrow night at the hotel. Do you want to come?"

"Much obliged, ma'am. But I'm heading out as well. Just you be sure to be on the 11:00 plane."

And he tipped his Stetson and drove off in a small cloud of dust.

A party was not an everyday occurrence at the Hotel Casa Paradiso. The regulars lived there cheaply and did not have funds for heavy entertaining. I asked Mario if I could hold a dinner there and he agreed to help me do it. His cousin Jorge would cater. I told Mario that I wanted boiled chicken for Marjorie, Blue Margaritas for everyone, a large cake, and anything else that seemed appropriate. The guests would be Mario, Rosa, the Professor, Marjorie, and Rodriguez, the bellboy. I couldn't think of anyone else who would want to come.

The party that night was a huge success. Not many of the invited guests often got an offer of free food and drink, and Mario, Rosa, and Rodriguez probably never got a chance to sit down and be served—even by Cousin Jorge.

The Blue Margaritas were especially appreciated. For me, they reminded me of my almost-night in Puerto Escondido with Michael. For the others, I guess, it was just a delicious drink, although I noticed the Professor quietly refilling his glass straight from the bottle of tequila rather than from the pitcher of margaritas.

Marjorie appreciated the boiled chicken in her honor and also my toast to the Oaxaca Library. I promised to send some shipments of used books at the first opportunity.

Rosa was somewhat quiet throughout but made a toast to El Coyote. "Long may he live in our hearts," she said in Spanish. We all raised our glasses.

The Professor made the last toast. "We'll miss you, Schaeffer Brown," he said, "but, as the poet Rilke says, 'Life is just a series of farewells.'"

36

Anima Sola

I WAS CHEWING OVER the words of the Professor's toast in my mind as the plane from Oaxaca took off from the small runway, over the huge plateau of south central Mexico amid the stately mountains. A short stop in Mexico City, a few naps, and a couple of devilishly hard crossword puzzles later, I was back at Dulles International Airport in McLean, Virginia. I found my ever-ready-to-start though interiorly frosty Jeep in the parking lot and made my way through the cold, damp landscape back to North Arlington. It was good to see my cozy yellow cottage, even though it was now a mite chilly till I cranked up the heat.

Of course, I spoke first with my client, Emily Crawford, and filled in the details. She was extremely grateful for my getting Courtney back safely and even glad that Montgomery (the bastard) had gotten his comeuppance and was languishing somewhere in a Mexican jail.

I also told her about how her first husband, Courtney's father, had played a key role in the affair. I added that he really seemed still to care very much about her (Emily) and was, of course, devoted to Courtney. I thought that I should put in a good word for Curtis here. He was an odd duck, what with his matchbook collection and his giant aquariums, but I really thought that he still carried a torch for Emily and that Courtney could use a firm parental hand. I made a note to myself to call Curtis, report in, and leave a distinct impression that a visit to Emily and Courtney would not be unwelcome.

I asked Emily how Courtney was doing and could I talk with her.

Emily said that Courtney was doing fine and currently out riding with the two Jessicas, who were spending the night. Youth are so resilient.

I told Emily that I would send her a full written report and an account of expenses by the end of the week. I warned her that the expenses would be hefty, but she seemed really grateful and even sounded as though she hadn't had a drink in a while. She seemed a lot happier than when I had seen her last.

I called in to work, too, and reached Marna, who was really glad to know that I was back. I gave her the short version of the events of the last days and vowed to fill in the details later.

Then I asked after Will. It was hard to believe but it had been little more than a week since the shooting, and Marna said that there was no change from his previous condition. He didn't open his eyes, he mumbled something infrequently, and was still mostly unconscious.

"Marna," I asked, "is Will supposed to get better?"

"I don't know, dear. The doctors can't say for sure. They say it could go either way. But he's a strong man, Schaeffer, and I know that he wants to live."

"Any ideas about who shot him?"

"Not yet. The police and we have come up blank."

Finally, I asked to speak with Michael. I had been holding myself back, trying not to be impatient.

"Actually, he and Anna went off for a day. Something therapeutic, Michael said. Michael will be back tomorrow though."

"Well, so will I," I said, trying to sound cheerful. "You can expect me in at nine o'clock—or maybe ten o'clock, realistically speaking..."

Finally, I called Rachel, my friend and lawyer, and left a message on her machine saying that I was back home and looking forward to seeing her.

After making these calls, I had no question about what I would do next. I had to see Will for myself. I quickly looked through my suitcase and found the tin pig ornament that I had bought for him to add to his collection. I would put it next to the pink quartz pig that I had left on his bedside table before leaving for Oaxaca. The pigs were whimsical and a little silly, yes, but they seemed to connect him in some way to his boyhood on the Iowa farm.

I had been thinking a lot about Will really, how much I cared for him, admired, and respected him. And I was trying to sort out whether these feelings were more those of a daughter or of a romantic sort. The unresolved quasi-incestuous nature of my feelings disturbed me, and I wanted to resolve them one way or the other. This was hard to do with Will lying in a hospital bed, fighting for his life.

It was only a little more than a week since I had left Will at Sibley Hospital. It seemed more like a month or a year. Everything had changed for me. I had experienced the color and exotic life of Mexico. I had concluded my first solo case. I had spent one romantic night with—well, near—Michael. I had fought for my life against a desperate and dangerous man with a large firearm. Most important was my newly discovered knowledge that I did take my life seriously, that I wanted to live and work and experience the world, and, yes, have another try at love.

At Sibley Hospital, though, all was depressingly still very much the same. There was the quiet reception area, the quiet corridors, the quiet nurses' station, and the quietly opening door to Will's room. How did hospital doors do that? I wondered idly. They didn't seem to have hinges or wheels or anything. They just opened silently.

But I was merely putting off my first sight of Will. I walked in slowly, afraid of what I would see. He was, in large part, as I had left him. He was lying on a hospital bed, slightly raised up, in a comfortable pale-yellow double room. Since the hospital was never full, he had no roommate.

My heart nearly broke seeing him so still there on the bed. He was meant to be vigorous, alive, moving, talking, chortling, smoking, drinking martinis, and hunting down evildoers. I could hardly stand to see him like this. The oxygen mask had been removed; he was clearly breathing on his own. But an IV in his right arm suggested that he was still being fed intravenously. This confirmed Marna's description of his near-comatose state.

I sat down on the edge of his bed. I spoke his name and took his hand, but got no response at all. In spite of myself, tears started to fall as if with a will of their own. Something inside clarified itself for me. Will was not my own dear father, who had died nearly 17 years ago. My father was loving and compassionate. He was light and full of wit and play. No, Will was not my father. No one could ever replace him. But I felt toward Will as I would toward a father. I wanted him to be proud of me, to love and protect me. Attractive as Will was, it wasn't in the end a romantic feeling I had for him. I knew that now. And still my heart was breaking for him.

"Will," I said, knowing that he couldn't hear me. "I think you would have been proud of me in Oaxaca. I think that Will Thompson Forensic Associates lived up to its reputation and your good name. I've learned so much from you, more than you could ever know. Thank you for taking me in when I needed a fresh start. I can never repay you, but I will always try." I paused. "Please, please get better, Will. We all need you."

I sat there for a while in silence. A nurse came in at one point, but saw nothing was needed and withdrew quietly. On the rolling table next to Will's bed was still the pink quartz pig. I put the tin Mexican pig beside it.

Finally I whispered a good-night, kissed Will's cheek, and left.

Epilogue

WHEN I RETURNED HOME from the hospital, I was feeling lonely and forlorn. But the little yellow cottage was definitely warming up now. I put on all of the lights and the radio for comfort. I began contemplating acquiring a cat for company. Perhaps I would get a black cat and see if it was my tono.

I next decided to throw all of my suitcase clothes in the washer and lay out all of my Oaxaca mementos on the kitchen table—at least the ones that had good associations. There was the matchbook from J. Gilbert's, my first clue, the Professor's calling card, my tin cow ornament, and the machete that Jesus helped me pick out at the Indian market, with the inscription that read, "Ay, my little sweetheart—do not use me to destroy our love."

Next I tried to encourage a cheerier mood by making myself some hot chocolate and pouring it into my favorite mug and helping myself to some formerly frozen Pepperidge Farm apple turnovers now baked to a golden brown.

I was just beginning to get cozy when I was startled to hear the doorbell ring. I wasn't expecting anyone and hoped it would be Michael. How lovely to share my cocoa and turnovers with him and fill him in on the details of my last days in Oaxaca. But this was not to be.

I walked to the door, stared through the peephole, and saw, in distorted fishbowl fashion, not Michael but my second ex-husband, Nick. Nick, you'll recall, was the English husband who, by stepping out with Roger in Accounting, had started me on my new career and new life.

To my surprise, I didn't exactly feel any hostility to him just then. I did feel something, though. It seemed to be a mixture of shock at seeing him after all this time; distress at having to deal with him; and maybe just a dash of nostalgia for our early good days together. It was a confusing emotion, intense and upsetting at the same time.

I unlocked the door and opened it. Immediately I knew that something was very, very wrong. Nick looked terrible: pale, unkempt, furtive, and very angry. I just stared.

"Can I come in?" he said.

"Well, sure," I said carefully. "Take off your wet coat. Would you like some hot chocolate? An apple turnover?"

He just stood there in his coat and stared at me. "You know that you ruined my life, don't you?" he said in his well-maintained English accent. His voice was hard and flat.

"I have no idea what you're talking about, Nick," I said a trifle hotly. "Neither of us may have contributed much to the marriage, but you were the one who was having an affair. I merely found out and let the law take its course."

"You told everyone. I became a laughing stock. I lost my job, and I haven't been able to find another one. No one in banking wanted to hire me."

"I'm sorry for you, really. But I didn't talk to anyone about you. It was way too humiliating for me," I said and meant it. "I just wanted to get the whole thing over with."

"You liar," he snarled. "I know that you set out to ruin me."

I knew, of course, that Nick had a very bad temper and that he threw things when he got angry. I remembered, near the end of our relationship, thinking that he might hurt me if he got mad enough. And then there were all of those angry phone calls and hang-ups. I knew that I should have been trying to calm him down, but something angry snapped in me, too.

"I don't have to listen to this," I broke in. "Why are you here, anyway?"

"To finish what I started about a week ago."

That gave me pause. I was beginning to get a glimmer of the situation here and also beginning to be seriously worried.

"You mean," I stammered, "that you tried to kill me last week near my car? That it was you? And you shot my boss by mistake? That was *you*?"

Nick just looked at me. "Well, actually, yes," Nick said finally with a really nasty trace of a smile. He was calming down all right, but it was an eerie kind of calm at best.

I was thinking back to that day. It was cold and snowy and I had given Will some quilts to wrap around him while he cleaned the ice off the car. Will was around my side of the car when he had been shot. Nick must have thought it was me.

Then I remembered that Will's only words since the shooting were "her husband." We all thought that Will meant Montgomery Crawford. But he had meant Nick. Will had figured it out and was trying to warn us, to protect me.

"Anyway," Nick continued, sounding really strange and loony, "drive-by revenge isn't satisfying at all. I wanted to do it face to face."

I started to back away towards the telephone and tried to slow things down, hoping that he would come to his senses. "But, Nick, how can you hate me so much? We were lovers once. We have history, good times together. I never meant you any harm or did you any harm."

"Yes. Right," he said, this time with irony. "And don't bother trying to get to the telephone, " he added crisply. "I took the precaution of cutting the wire outside while you were out."

I stopped and stared at him.

"Now," Nick added, almost playfully, "how shall I finish you off? It needs to be slow and painful so that I can feel your suffering. I don't suppose you bothered to feel mine. .." he mused. "There's bleeding slowly to death. That's good, but messy."

I just couldn't believe this. I knew that Nick had been acting unstable, but now he seemed to have crossed some clearly marked line into insanity. I started moving toward the kitchen's back door.

"I wouldn't bother trying to get there either," Nick said coolly. "I also disabled the latch from the outside. It's completely impassable."

I began to feel trapped and dangerously close to panic.

"But, as I was saying, I want you to feel, really feel, my pain. And I was thinking, as well as I know you, that what would really hurt you is to tap into your well-known claustrophobia. For example," he said, warming to his subject, "I could tie you up, slit your wrists, and lock you in your ghastly hope chest that you're so proud of. As if Americans had anything to call an antique. Then you could scare yourself to death, or bleed to death, or both. And it would be much less messy."

I just stood there in silence, stunned. Of course, Nick was well aware of my worst fears. I could imagine myself in my hope chest, in the dark, unable to get the lid open, the sides of the chest closing in on me. I would scream for help and Nick would just laugh. I would feel the air being used up, feel myself beginning to suffocate. I would gasp for air and at the same time feel my blood seeping away and smell its sickening sweetness. For me, no death could be crueler.

At that moment, Nick pulled a strong-looking cord from his coat pocket and came towards me, making me back up into the kitchen. He was evidently going to tie me up first. I knew that he was stronger than I was, but I certainly wasn't going down without a fight. I had learned some new moves in P.I. school since Nick and I had last quarreled.

But Nick moved first. As he backed me into the kitchen table, his right fist suddenly came at my mouth and knocked me to the floor. I felt a sickening crack in my jaw and the awful sound of teeth breaking. The pain was surprisingly not terrible, but I could see that I was bleeding badly and was scared, unprepared for this surprise move. I fell hard, back against the kitchen table, and somehow pulled the kitchen tablecloth down with me, with the hot chocolate, the turnovers, and the mementos of Oaxaca.

As Nick came toward me with the cord in his hands, I once again felt the paralyzing fear that I had felt in Oaxaca. But I knew that I needed to snap out of it if I didn't want to die. I have something to live for, I said to myself. I will not let Nick kill me. Remembering suddenly, I reached back behind me and groped for my souvenir machete, which had to be on the floor. I grasped it in my right hand, keeping it behind me and waiting for the right moment.

"Oh, and one more thing," Nick said, standing above me and fingering his rope. "I decided to finish off your lover Will Thompson, too."

"I don't believe you," I said slowly, gasping through the blood now filling up my mouth.

"Yes, really. I followed you to Sibley Hospital just now. I smothered him with a pillow just after you left."

"I don't believe you," I stammered again.

"No?" said Nick with sudden anger. "Then where did I get these?" He reached into his coat pocket and took out the pink quartz pig and the tin Mexican one. He threw them at me with disgust. "I really couldn't take the chance that he would come to and figure it all out. Besides, any friend of yours..."

I did not know that I was capable of feeling such rage. It overwhelmed me and energized me at the same time. With this new-found strength and every ounce of pent-up anger, I lurched to my feet and whipped the machete as hard as I could across Nick's throat. It felled him, and he sank to the floor in a pool of blood.

I still don't remember getting to the hospital. My neighbors tell me that I walked out my front door and banged on theirs, asking them to call 911. I was bleeding badly and still clutching the small machete that Jesus Montoya had helped me buy. The inscription seemed somewhat more apt when I learned that Nick had died that night, there on my kitchen floor.

Well, I didn't make it in to work the next day at 9:00 or 10:00 either. What Nick had told me about Will was true. He was dead. Marna and Michael closed the office for the next week, notified Will's family, and made funeral arrangements. They both came out to see me as soon as they could. They cleaned and straightened up my cottage, bought me groceries, and made me soft foods to eat—chicken soup, chocolate pudding, and red Jell-O. My jaw had a hairline fracture that would have to heal on its own. I also had a badly split lip that now had 18 stitches in it, and two cracked teeth, which would need to have some major dental work to hold them together.

Michael and Marna tried to comfort me about Will's death, but they were deeply saddened themselves. I wanted to talk with Michael alone, but he smoothed my brow and whispered, "Later."

Rachel came and took care of me, too. For about a week, she spent time with me every day. Although talking was difficult for me, Rachel loved hearing a little about the events in Oaxaca. I couldn't talk at all about Will or about my last encounter with Nick. It was too painful. But Rachel said that she was glad to know me, that I had done our sex and my new calling proud.

In a week or so, I started to heal, and, as I got my strength back, my spirits began to revive a little. I was able to get to Will's memorial service, which was packed with friends and grateful clients. Will's father and mother were too frail to come from Iowa, but his younger brother Don was there. He had a disconcerting likeness to the Will I had first met, the same grin, the same blue eyes, the same warm handshake.

Michael, Marna, and I sat together at the service. Anna wasn't there but that might only mean that she was on a fact-finding mission to Senegal or somewhere else exotic. As we were leaving, Michael pulled me aside and took my hand.

"You know, we have a whole lot of private investigation left to do together, mi amiga," he said. "We've only just begun."

I held on to that thought as I got into my trusty Jeep and drove home.

◗ CANDACE KATZ is Deputy Director of the President's Committee on the Arts and the Humanities. She holds a Ph.D. in English from Harvard University, a J.D. from Georgetown University, and is a registered Private Investigator in the Commonwealth of Virginia.